MIKE RIPLEY

Mike Ripley is the author of six Angel novels, as well as numerous short stories. He is twice winner of the Crime Writers' Association's Last Laugh award for funniest crime novel of the year.

He is crime critic for the *Daily Telegraph* and has written scripts for both radio and television, including the BBC's *Lovejoy* series.

A Yorkshireman by birth, he has worked in the brewing industry in London since 1978. He lives with his wife and three children in a converted farmhouse in East Anglia. The Aga is on order.

REVIEWS OF ANGEL CITY

'Exuberant, laugh-aloud fun and cleverness... but there is, in addition, an edge and an anger'

MARCEL BERLINS, *The Times*

'Hugely funny, with a catch in ~~the~~ ... politicians should steer cle~~ar~~ ... ~~Ri~~pley as he cuts through ...

... ~~Ob~~server

'Enough succes~~s~~ ... ~~te~~levision comic going until ...

T.J. BINYON, *Daily Telegraph*

'A wonderfully evocative book, with the comic thriller elements nicely balanced'

JEREMY J. BEADLE, *Gay Times*

By the same author

ANGEL CONFIDENTIAL
ANGEL CITY
ANGELS IN ARMS
ANGEL TOUCH
JUST ANOTHER ANGEL

MIKE RIPLEY

Angel City

HarperCollins*Publishers*

HarperCollins*Publishers*
77–85 Fulham Palace Road,
Hammersmith, London W6 8JB

This paperback edition 1995
1 3 5 7 9 8 6 4 2

First published in Great Britain by
HarperCollins*Publishers* 1994

Copyright © Mike Ripley 1994

The Author asserts the moral right to
be identified as the author of this work

ISBN 0 00 649012 3

Set in Meridien and Bodoni

Printed in Great Britain by
HarperCollinsManufacturing Glasgow

1

I was having breakfast sitting on the back of a borrowed Kawasaki in Porter Street, but only because they'd removed the picnic benches from outside the Burger King opposite, when I first met Tigger O'Neil.

Once those benches had gone, the early morning shift of dispatch riders had deserted the Burger King for the McDonald's just across Baker Street, parking their bikes round the corner in Porter Street. Those with mobile phones ate inside the Mac; those, like me, with tin-pot North Korean radios had to stay outside to get the reception. As a rule, there would be four or five of us there each morning on the Red Eye shift between seven a.m. and eight a.m., struggling with the first Egg McMuffin of the day and clutching environmentally friendly (well, almost) cups of coffee, trying to stay one degree above hypothermia.

The main topic of intellectual conversation was to look up Baker Street to the traffic lights across the Marylebone Road and try and guess which of the outlaw car-wash operators would score. That set of lights is one of the longest time-lags in west London and attracts a fair number of students from the polytechnic with plastic buckets of cold, filthy water and usually one of those plastic ice-scrapers you can buy from garages for under a quid. The trick was to pick on the front two rows of cars stuck at the lights, dive out and start swilling water on to their windscreens. Most motorists, or at least those with a small BMW or above, paid up straight away in order to get rid of them. Some yelled abuse, some sank down in their seats and pretended it wasn't happening. The trick for the washer was not to get too far out into the road as when the lights did change, there were always a few

7

hard-case boy racers who looked on them as legitimate targets and tried not to take prisoners.

There were about a dozen of them working that morning, which meant that their student grants must have been late arriving as it was still early in the term. They had formed a rota system and seemed to be milking the traffic reasonably successfully, and the only laughs they offered us was when a big Rover swerved slightly to clip one of the buckets left too near the edge of the pavement, sending it spinning out into the cross traffic like a wayward football.

One of the students made as if to run out into Marylebone Road to retrieve it, but another held him back.

'Aw, let 'im play in the traffic,' shouted the Beast, then laughed mirthlessly.

The lights changed and the cross traffic surged like they were recording sound effects for Le Mans. The bucket got bounced by one of the flash, low-slung Citroëns and went under the wheels of a truck carrying fruit-flavoured yog-hurts, the sort probably most popular among students at the polytechnic.

The Beast turned away, the morning's entertainment over for him, and offered me a cigarette. I took one even though I was determined to give up and normally didn't smoke before nightfall anyway. I took one because the Beast might have been offended if I hadn't.

I think his given name was Tony, which only posed the question who would give him a name at all. I found it difficult to imagine any parental couple, however broody, however Christian, however desperate, ever actually owning up to him. The other riders called him the Beast from the East, because he came from East Ham, though never to his face. Normally, he came across as a sexist, racist, homophobic thug who had once seriously tried to fit open Swiss army pen-knives to the spokes of his motor bike. But then on some days he could be really unpleasant.

'Thanks, Tone,' I said, taking a Marlboro and checking that his lighter was on a low gas setting before leaning into it for a light. (Rule of Life No. 93: Sometimes you can never be too careful.) 'Another coffee?'

'Yeah, four sugars. No, wait, it's my shout,' he growled.

He took my cup from me and started round the corner, then remembered he wasn't taking glasses back to the bar, so he dropped them. They rustled down Baker Street until they fetched up against a City of Westminster litter bin.

I wondered what I was doing sitting there watching paper cups gently biodegrade at that time of the morning, in the company of morons like the Beast.

Oh yes, now I remember. It's called *work*.

It was the worst of times, it was the shittiest of times. There was a recession on. You could tell that from the way the government denied it. What was worse, it was hitting London instead of some far-flung northern city where they had much more experience of handling such things, and it was doing so after a decade of ultra-positive attitudes to getting rich quick. Even if there had never been a realistic chance of it, there was also the hope that around the corner lay a yet flashier BMW.

What was serious was that the economic nutcracker was squeezing the really important industries: advertising agencies, marketing and public relations consultants, the pubs, jobbing printers, the video production companies. The very areas where you could pick up a bit of work if you had to pay the rent.

I had to, because I was skint. The old cash-flow had not so much flowed but done a tidal race out to sea. Times were hard and looked like getting harder in the Big Plum.

The Big Plum?

London; because there's a very hard stone at the centre.

'Oscar Seven. Oscar Seven.'

I ambled over to where I'd parked Armstrong and picked up the radio from the driver's seat.

Armstrong is a black London cab of the old school, the Austin FX4S, a vehicle tailor-made for London traffic from a design inspired by the Panzer sweeps across Russia in 1941. He's delicensed, of course, and there is no longer room on the clock for enough zeroes to record the number of miles he's done. There is nothing wrong with owning one, though for obvious reasons, very few get sold off second- or third-hand in London itself. I've disconnected the yellow roof light which says TAXI and where the old fare meter used to be, there is now a tape deck rigged up to my own ICE design – In-Cab Entertainment. So I'm not really trying to pass myself off as anything, certainly not a real musher who's done the knowledge, but it is amazing how many people get the wrong idea.

'Oscar bloody Seven, come in. Earth to Planet Oscar, are you receiving?'

'Yeah, yeah, yeah. Get on with it.'

I had no patience with the mob back at Dispatch. I mean, here I was with a cab called Armstrong and my name Angel and what do I get as a call sign? Oscar bloody Seven.

'You anywhere near Crumpet Central?'

'Could be,' I answered.

Crumpet Central was the name given to Euston Square tube station by the dispatch riding fraternity, especially over the air where they had code names for key locations in case an opposition firm was listening in. Why Crumpet Central? Because someone with nothing better to do had once sat down and worked out that eighty-four per cent of the passengers arriving at Euston Square during the morning rush hour were women, mostly aged between twenty and twenty-five. With the recession, all the good jobs like that had gone, naturally.

'The Fly-By Ad Agency on Gower Street have a package for the BBC, Portland Place. Pick up at eight-thirty, deliver by nine,' said Dispatch like it was his mantra.

'Know it,' I replied wearily. 'Goods only, or passenger and goods?'

'Just said package in name of Barton. That's B for Bastard, A for . . .'

'I can spell. This is Oscar Seven, not Hammer One.'

Hammer One was the call sign of the Beast from the East. He'd been allowed to choose his own as no one would argue with him.

'Well, it's just a parcel. Artwork by the sound of it. And

get a timed signature to prove it's there before nine. Roger?'

'Angels One Five,' I said to confuse him and clicked the radio off, dropping it back on to Armstrong's driver's seat.

Another piddling job. An advertising agency on a promise with somebody at the BBC had screwed up an overnight job and were finishing their artwork before start of business there – in most areas, about ten-fifteen a.m. The agency couldn't take any chances, say on it raining and the stuff getting wet, so they'd booked a cab rather than a bike. They wouldn't take it themselves because if it didn't make it on time, they had someone else to blame. They also preferred a cab because the drivers don't wear crash helmets and can be identified more easily. Therefore they're more likely to hang around and actually get somebody to sign for the package. The riders usually nip in, throw it down and dive out. Sometimes they get the right building. In fact, it's only recently that banks and building societies have insisted on bikers removing their helmets before entering so the video cameras can clock them.

It was my first job of the day and given the split I was on with the dispatch company, would just about cover the cost of breakfast. Just about. Thank God they don't expect tips in McDonald's.

I checked my Seastar and found I had over half an hour to go and it would only take me five minutes to get to Fly-By on Gower Street. Having taken the job, though, I was stuck in the West One area unless something else turned up very local. With my luck lately, there'd be a call out for a run to Heathrow (good for twenty pounds usually) and I wouldn't be able to take it as I'd be shunting between Gower Street and Broadcasting House.

It was crazy. You could virtually see Portland Place from Gower Street. Well, you could if the Post Office Tower wasn't in the way. And for this sort of money?

I was depressed.

The Beast reappeared with two cups of steaming coffee. He'd forgotten the lids.

I began to think of good philosophical justification for suicide. His.

11

Two other riders in full leathers followed him out. One I knew as Crimson, a tall black teenager from a rival firm and the best, most natural bike rider I'd seen in a long time. The other worked for the same company, but was a new face to me.

The Beast handed me a cup and straddled his machine. For the first time I noticed he had put HAMMER ONE on his petrol tank in the kind of stick-on lettering you normally see on the gates of bungalows in seaside resorts. He probably used it as an *aide-mémoire*.

Crimson flashed a killer look at the back of the Beast's head and I gave a shrug of the shoulders in response.

'How ya doin', Angel?' Crimson asked, giving the Beast and his bike the widest berth the pavement would allow.

The kid with him did a little skip and shuffle, almost a dance step, and ran a gauntlet finger over the rear mudguard of the Beast's Kawasaki as if looking for dust. The Beast didn't see that but he did see Crimson and his lip twisted so much it wouldn't fit round his styrofoam cup.

'Struggling on, Crimson, struggling on.'

'You, struggling? Get outa here.'

'It's true. And it's true what they say: life's a bitch, then you die.'

'Man, you are down and I mean pits.' He rested an elbow on Armstrong's bonnet. I had to turn to look at him. The kid with him skipped around to stand behind him. It seemed he couldn't keep still for more than two seconds.

'Why the concern?' I asked, genuinely puzzled. Crimson was a nodding acquaintance, no more.

'Interested in some work?'

'A bit of moooonlighting . . .' whispered the kid loudly, executing a fair Michael Jackson toe tap and twirl through one hundred and eighty degrees.

I frowned at Crimson.

'This is Tigger,' Crimson said sheepishly.

The kid held up one finger of his right hand to his forehead.

'Hello, Tigger,' I said and he put his hand behind his head

and did another soft-shoe dance step over the cracks in the pavement.

'What's up with that ponce?' snarled the Beast.

'Aerobics, Tony,' I said over my shoulder.

Crimson nodded towards Armstrong. I got the message.

'Come in out of the cold and we'll blag,' I said.

As I moved towards the offside door, Crimson bundled Tigger into the back through the nearside. I had my hand on the rumble seat when the Beast yelled out.

'Hey, Angel, I went down the greengrocer's on Saturday an' I was gonna buy my mum a lovely bunch of grapes till I saw they was from South Africa. I told 'em, I'm not buying South African. What? The thought of all those black bastards handling yer fruit, makes yer flesh crawl.'

'Fine, Tony, good one,' I said as I slammed the door. I was facing Crimson, our knees touching. 'Ignore him. He's just bragging that he's got a mother after all.'

'He doesn't get to me,' said Crimson, who had certainly heard worse.

'He gets to me,' said Tigger, pulling down the other folding seat and plonking his feet on it.

I looked at his feet, crossed Nike trainers that had seen better yesterdays. Then I looked up slowly into his face. He held it for a few seconds, then pulled his feet off and let the seat slap back up.

I turned back to Crimson.

'So?'

'Tigger here's got a job offer, driving. It's no good to me 'cos it's night work.'

'And, don't tell me, your aura is sunlight. You're a Day Person.'

'What?'

'Sorry, don't mind me. I must be feeling my New Age.' He didn't look any wiser. 'Skip it. Why don't you want it? Is it hooky?'

'It's legit, but maybe non-union if you get my drift,' Tigger chipped in. He was crossing and uncrossing his legs rapidly, his leather riding suit creaking in rhythm. The guy could fidget for England at the Olympics.

13

'So why not you?' I said to Crimson, ignoring the Kid.

'Because I'm busy most nights with my partner and anyway, I ain't got an HGV. You have.'

I did indeed have a Heavy Goods Vehicle driver's licence. Moreover, it was in my real name, unlike some of my others, and was therefore precious.

'OK, so it's lorry work. What are we shifting and how far? I'm not into S & D you know.'

Crimson knew what I meant, but I wasn't sure Tigger did. It must have made him think, for every part of his body was still for almost half a minute.

'Stand and Deliver,' Crimson told him. 'Lorry drivers who grass their routes to the villains and then go along with a bit of highway robbery for a cut later on.'

'It's nothing like that,' said Tigger and I believed him because he started fidgeting again. 'This is strictly inner city driving and the cargo has no retail value.'

He'd heard that somewhere and I wondered where.

'So what's the catch?'

'No catch I know of, except you take me as driver's mate.'

'Why?'

'Because I can't drive at all, my Angel.' He lisped this and flicked a wrist at my knee, all the time watching my face. 'Is that really your name?'

'Is yours Tigger?'

'Tigger O'Neil, that's me. I'm going to be famous one day.'

'I'll bet you already are in some quarters,' I said.

'Ain't that the fact of it,' Crimson agreed.

Tigger dropped the camp act.

'Look, you don't have to like me, but I'm the one who can get you in on this. I'll load and unload, you drive. That's fair, isn't it? Crimson here suggested you and that's good enough for me.'

I was also convenient, sitting just round the corner, but I didn't say anything.

'And it pays a hundred a night – each. We can get maybe three jobs a week. Regular work, see. Now if you're in, say so.'

'I'll think about it.'

Crimson put his hand on the door handle.

'Sort it out amongst yourselves, girls.'

'How do I find you?' I asked Tigger.

'You don't. Nobody finds me. There's a pub called the Grapes in Rimmer Road over in Bow. Know it?'

'I could find it.'

'Then be there at eight tonight and meet the man who gives out the pay packets. See you then. Remember, eight till late, bring a crate.'

He flashed out a hand and had the door open and closed behind him in a trice. Crimson and I watched open-mouthed as he went up on ballet dancer points and skipped right up to where the Beast sat on his bike.

Tigger did a pirouette, arms out. He bowed, blew a kiss from the palm of his hand at the Beast, then jumped over the bike, his right foot bouncing off the seat perilously close to the Beast's crotch.

He didn't look back, just landed and started running right out into Baker Street where he hopped aboard a Number 13 bus.

The Beast was too stunned to move, his cup of coffee still halfway to his mouth. Then he yelled 'Oi!' and started to climb off the bike but by then the bus was gone.

'It might be diplomatic not to mention that in the Beast's hearing,' I said.

'You know me, man. I'm all for the quiet life,' said Crimson.

Something puzzled me. Tigger had been dressed like a dispatch rider, right down to the chest ponchos they give you with the name of the company on.

'Where's Tigger's bike?'

'Oh, he don't have a bike,' said Crimson. 'He just likes wearing leather.'

They say that all the commissionaires at Broadcasting House are hired because they are war veterans. The trouble is nobody knows which war.

I had picked up my assigned package dead on time from the Fly-By Ad Agency. In fact, I had been early, as Zandra the receptionist had pointed out. The package was indeed artwork; Zandra was between commitments, a Taurean and ate lunch in the vegetarian wine bar round the corner.

I made it to the BBC in fifteen minutes, parked on double yellows round the corner as if I was waiting for custom from the hotel there, and then spent twenty-five minutes trying to get somebody to sign a receipt for the package.

When one of the uniforms eventually agreed to take on this massive responsibility, he insisted on putting the time in as 0911 hours and he did it in green ink. That meant I would have to buy a green pen in order to fiddle it to prove it had arrived before nine, which it had.

That, I decided, I could do without as by then I would be making a loss on the job.

More than anything, I suppose that got me thinking about Tigger's offer of work. However shady, it had to be better than arguing the dawn away with BBC commissionaires and then Dispatch – and all for the difference between two quid or four quid or whatever the going rate was for on-time deliveries.

The morning didn't get any better. There was the incident with the traffic warden near Goodge Street tube station. Then there was the dipstick from an oil company who wanted taking to Lydford Road, W9, only to find, halfway there, that it should have been Lydeard Road, E6, but he wasn't going to pay the extra. And then there was having to take a crate of live racing pigeons from a very strange house in Fulham to King's Cross in order to Red Star them to Doncaster. Or should it have been Warrington? I was past caring.

By lunch time, I was ready to sign off, go home, grab some sleep and see what Tigger came up with that evening.

I thought then, and went on thinking, that he was called Tigger because he never stopped moving. I didn't realize then that his real name was Christopher Robin O'Neil.

I didn't find out until I read the report of his inquest in the local paper.

2

I got home to Hackney by mid-afternoon and made the first constructive decision of the day: to move.

I have shared a house at 9 Stuart Street for longer than I like to think. I was getting to be the longest-serving resident and there seemed to be no remission for bad behaviour. Nowadays I was actually getting letters there and I wasn't that keen to hear from people I didn't know who could write. They have this habit of using recycled brown envelopes with little windows in and funny initials usually starting 'H.M.'. What was worse, the junk mail had started to arrive addressed to me personally. That afternoon alone I had won a Ford Fiesta (on condition I bought two tons of concrete in a Spanish timeshare), was being invited to become a mail-order catalogue agent (and claim my free gadget for grating carrots nine million ways) and had three envelopes in which to return my holiday snapshots in the faint hope that the right film would be returned to me that year, if I was lucky. When the junk fliers catch up on you, it is time to show a large proportion of leg and do a runner.

Why not? Everyone else seemed to be on the move. Except the mysterious Mr Goodson from the ground-floor flat, that is. We didn't really know about him. He came, he went, he was something in local government. What he did behind his permanently closed door we didn't know, but he didn't annoy any of the rest of us, so we let him be. I occasionally imagined he might have an alternative existence as a spy, or moonlighted as Miss Whiplash offering personal services to Cabinet Ministers. Or maybe he was a member of the Cabinet.

In the flat above mine, the Celtic Twilight were about to

move, though it seemed like they'd only been there two minutes. I had called them the Celtic Twilight in case they ever formed a folk group. If they had, it would only have been with the intention of cheering up Leonard Cohen.

My first impression of them – Inverness Doogie and his Welsh wife Miranda – was that they had both been taking the humourless pills too long. They smiled about as often as every other census and for a comedian like me, they were the audience from hell. Still, they had their plus points. Doogie was a very good man to have in a scrap, on your side, that is, streetfighting being his main interest after his job as a chef working his way up the pastry career ladder. Miranda was a journalist on local weekly papers in north London, which wouldn't normally endear her to me. But, give her her due, she had sneaked in a couple of free small ads so I could get rid of a coven of kittens to good homes – one of which had even insisted on paying for one, and I must give Miranda her cut one of these days.

The kittens were an unexpected Christmas present – well, more of a paternity suit really – from a man in the same street who had tried to breed Siamese cats and had been doing OK until Springsteen, with whom I happen to share Flat three, had gone round to pay his respects.

Once weaned, the kittens had been dumped on me and it had taken ages for me to dump them on unsuspecting homes in north London, even though my odd aunt Dorothea took the three biggest and most vicious, as she was convinced that a new strain of attack cats was the coming thing once they banned Rottweilers.

To be honest, I'd used a similar line with some of the other punters who'd responded to the ad in the local paper. Somebody had actually worked out that cats killed around seventy million small mammals and birds a year in the UK alone. The odds on you surviving to see your pension if you were a wood mouse, a field vole or a house sparrow were not good. But, let's face it, when did you ever see a field vole in a betting shop? ('I didn't know they raced voles,' one of the respondents to the ad had said, dead straight. She ended up with a pair of kittens and it served her right.)

18

But the traumatic exodus of the kittens paled alongside the prospect of the departure – or threatened departure – of Lisabeth and Fenella, the inhabitants of Flat Two, the one below mine.

Describing them is difficult, but a transvestite snorting coke while watching a Laurel and Hardy film would know what I meant immediately. They were also downright inconsiderate in that if two out of four flats became vacant, now that Doogie was going back to his roots to work in some posh country hotel in Scotland, then our landlord Nassim Nassim was quite likely to start reviewing his property portfolio. That could mean yours truly out on the streets and all because Lisabeth and Fenella had this really selfish notion that they needed a brighter, more positive aura than that offered by Hackney.

It had all started when Lisabeth had read a book called *The Midwife of Light*, or similar, and decided that Glastonbury was the only place to be. Fenella had tried to be enthusiastic about the mythical significance of it all and had gone in for homeopathic medicines in a big way. She'd even tried to teach herself acupuncture and for a while I thought she'd scuppered the whole plan, but Lisabeth did eventually manage to stop the bleeding and forgave her after being pacified with a red suede spell-pouch to wear round her neck and a jumbo-size bar of milk chocolate. Then I thought I had talked them out of it when I found an old AA road map and, late one night after even the pubs I use were shut, I showed them the dotted lines which proved that London, and especially Hackney, were surrounded by concentric ley lines thus making it the aura capital of the world.

For a couple of days they had been prepared to stay, at least until the end of the age of Aquarius, but then somebody had told them that I had been tracing the line of what was better known as the M25 orbital motorway, and they didn't speak to me for a week.

From the outside, it struck me that the Grapes in Rimmer Road was actually short for *The Grapes of Wrath*. It wasn't, of course, but I bet that's what the locals called it come Friday night.

I was early, so I had my pick of space in the car park, or rather the deserted building site next to the pub, leaving Armstrong near the entrance pointing out to facilitate a quick exit (Rule of Life No. 277).

It was a big 1930s roadside boozer with three bars, which had somehow escaped the Blitz even though people with taste had shone searchlights on it and yelled 'Over here!' to the bombers overhead. One bar had been retained as a Public Bar and Games Room and there were stickers in the frosted windows advertising eight-ball pool. Even from outside I could hear the mechanical chunter of fruit machines and a pinball machine.

The two original Lounge Bars had been knocked together into one huge drinking area, something usually regarded as heresy by pub-going traditionalists. In fact, pubs only had one bar until the seventeenth century when stagecoach travel (and then railways) introduced the concept of first- and second-class passengers. The first-class bods had to have a better bar at the staging posts – the pubs – along the road, so they would use the *salon*, the posh room, of the publican's house while those hanging on to the roof rack for dear life had to slum it in the bar with the locals. Hence, two-bar pubs and the word 'saloon', though not many people know that. Not many people give a toss about it, come to think of it.

If the internal dimensions of the pub had changed, then much of its furnishing had retained its character. The paint-work was beautifully nicotined and only slightly greasy to the touch, a few of the ashtrays had been emptied at least once and some of the longer slashes in the upholstery had been tastefully repaired with black insulating tape. The trouble was the locals would probably rise up in arms if anyone tried to change it or even remove one of the corny notices ranged behind the bar. Talk about kitsch, these were unfunny when they first came out. There were the tradit-ional ones such as DON'T TAKE OUR GLASSES, SEE AN OPTIC-IAN, and perennial favourites such as DON'T ASK FOR CREDIT

20

AS REFUSAL OFTEN OFFENDS and WE DON'T CASH CHEQUES EVEN GOOD ONES.

There was one which caught my eye which said, in relatively small print: IF YOU THINK YOU'VE BEEN GIVEN SHORT MEASURE PLEASE ASK FOR THE MANAGER — HE WILL BE PLEASED TO TELL YOU TO FUCK OFF.

But my favourite was the one truly original one, pinned to the fake wooden beam above the bar saying: GAY NIGHT LASER KARAOKE SHOWS — TUESDAYS AND THURSDAYS.

I smiled at that and ordered a bottle of lager. While the barman was struggling to take the top off, I leaned against the bar and looked around. I spotted three more of the signs advertising the gay karaoke nights.

They were serious.

I figured I had spotted the Man Who Gives Out the Pay Packets, as Tigger had called him, at least fifteen minutes before Tigger bothered to turn up.

I had started to relax once I remembered it was a Wednesday, even trying to engage the barman — an Irish lad not long enough away from the boreen to have stopped worrying about missing confession – in conversation.

'Popular, are they, these karaoke nights?' I'd opened.

'Oh, sure, yes. We have all the proper equipment you know.'

'If you don't have the equipment, it's called being drunk and disorderly,' I'd said and he'd thought about that until another customer had distracted him.

While he was down the other end of the bar I borrowed his *Evening Standard*, but it was open at the 'Situations Vacant' page, so I replaced it and found a seat at an empty table.

The pub was filling slowly, the going-home-from-work crowd being replaced by the going-up-West-for-the-night mob who needed lubrication before the minicabs arrived.

One guy was well out of place. He was about mid-fifties, short, with black, swept-back hair and a black moustache. He wore thick, square, black-framed glasses which made him blink every three seconds. I timed him. There was nothing else to do.

21

Sure enough, when Tigger did arrive just as I had decided not to invest in another beer and maybe give the whole thing a miss, he flounced straight by me and sat himself next to the guy in glasses.

'Umberto!' he squeaked, or at least that's what it sounded like, as he took one of the bloke's hands in his. The guy didn't look too keen on him borrowing it and he eased the grip free and stood up, saying something and nodding at the bar.

'Large Southern Comfort 'n' coke for me,' Tigger announced, then looked across at me. 'And another beer for my chauffeur.'

The older guy stared at me long enough to blink twice, then went for the drinks. Tigger waved me over.

He had changed out of his bike-rider's leathers into a light blue tracksuit and trainers. He perched rather than sat on his chair, folding his legs up under him in a semi-lotus position, and dragged another chair by the arm so I could be close to him.

'Has Umberto been here long?'

'Hadn't noticed,' I lied.

'I don't think you miss much, Angel,' he said loudly and reached out to pat my knee.

'How old are you, Tigger?' I asked to throw him, and it did for a millisecond.

'Nineteen. Why? Do I look younger?'

'No. Just surprised you made it that far.'

A bottle of Mexican beer thumped down on the table in front of me. There was a huge wedge of lemon balanced precariously in the top.

'The barman said everybody drinks these during Happy Hour,' said Umberto. 'And he said sorry about the lime as well. Wouldn't give me a glass, though.'

'I'll manage,' I said, flicking the lemon into the ashtray.

'Umberto Bassotti, this is Angel, but I don't think he likes me calling him that.'

'Roy will do.'

I nodded at Bassotti and he raised a glass at me. There was Scotch in it.

'Call me Bert, not Umberto, and don't for fuck's sake ask me what bit of Italy I come from.'

'Sicily, it's gotta be,' said Tigger immediately.

'Tuscany,' I said, joining in. There were so many people from Hampstead owning property in Tuscany now, it was known as Chiantishire and no genuine Italian in England would admit to coming from there.

'Pompeii? Pinocchio? AC Milan . . . ?' Tigger rattled on.

'I said not to ask, but if you must know, it's Bedford. I've never been to Italy, red wine gives me an 'eadache, pasta rots my guts and I couldn't name the Pope if you paid me. Now if that's out of the way, is the rest of the evening my own?'

Tigger put on a fake hurt look. I grinned and took a pull on the neck of my beer.

'You're gonna be our driver, then?' Bert said to me.

'I need the work,' I said, though the words didn't come out easily.

'What have you driven before?'

'Rock bands, dry goods, wet goods, a petrol tanker once. Oh yeah, and I used to do the Spitalfields grape run to Bedford, would you believe?' I said and all of it was true.

Bert raised his eyebrows and sipped more whisky.

'Bedford?' Tigger asked.

'The Italian community there used to buy up the remains of the Italian grape harvest from the old London fruit markets and turn them into wine. Kept them going for the next year.'

'Like home brewing, you mean?'

'Too right,' Bert chipped in. 'They'd invite you round to their houses and there'd be piles of bloody grapes in the bath. Get your shoes and socks off and start trampling. Bloody peasants. They'd make gallons of the stuff. Why they couldn't pop down the off-licence I don't know.'

'Was it legal?' chirped Tigger.

Bert and I exchanged pitying looks.

'Well, this isn't fresh fruit, Roy,' Bert went on, ignoring Tigger who had started fidgeting again.

'What exactly are we shifting; and where, and when?'

Bert looked at me, then at Tigger, who gave him a slight nod.

'Got a load waiting to go tonight if you're interested. It's not far away, and it goes as far as Barking.'

That wasn't very far at all. Not far enough to hire a driver and van unless there was something very dodgy about the cargo.

Tigger was making money signs, rubbing his forefinger and thumb together.

'Cash?'

'In hand. A ton each.'

'And if we're caught, we've never seen you before in our lives?'

'Me who? I'm at home watching the football on the telly.' He sipped from his drink and added: 'I hate football. The Eyeties are mad on it.'

'So what's the cargo?' I asked, knowing I'd regret it.

'A load of crap.'

It was a white box van. Well, of course, it would be. The ubiquitous, anonymous, dirty white box-backed van used to transport most of the stolen goods in London. The Model T Ford of the criminal classes and probably big enough to get a Model T in the back if you could find one.

It was parked nose first in a lock-up garage at the end of a street where unimproved Victorian terrace houses sprawled along one side down to the Stratford railway line and down the other, mid-size tower blocks of shoddily built Sixties flats offered panoramic views over the Grand Union Canal. It was so obviously a dodgy location I'm surprised the police didn't use it in their training films.

Bert Bassotti didn't help by looking furtively up and down the street before opening the first of three padlocks which held the doors. He looked like he'd done an Ealing Comedy acting course by post: Stock Character No. 31 – London shifty crook/spiv.

Tigger had ridden with him from the pub in an ageing Ford Sierra and I had followed, parking behind them down the street a few yards. Not dead outside the lock-up, I noted, but close enough to make a run for it if need be.

Bassotti got the doors open and disappeared inside. A second later, a weak low-wattage light came on. Tigger and I joined him, Tigger easing the door closed behind me.

'Can you drive one of these?' asked Bassotti.

'Has it got wheels?' I said.

'The keys are in. You're going over towards Creekmouth down by Barking. Know how to get there?'

'Out of here, on to Bow Road, after the hospital and the police station' – he winced at that – 'hang a right on to the Blackwall Tunnel approach then cut off towards Barking before you hit the East India Docks. After that, follow your nose.'

'After that, you follow Tigger. He knows exactly where to go. There's no rush. After midnight's better anyway. Tigger knows what to do. When he's dumped the stuff, bring the van back here and just snap the top padlock. Drop Tigger off wherever he wants to go.' He finished his speech and started edging towards the door.

'Hang on a sec,' I smiled. 'I might drive a taxi but I ain't on duty.'

'Tigger'll have your wages,' he said.

'Well that's different. Where to, sir?'

Tigger pulled his tracksuit top together over his chest and put on his orphan-in-the-storm look.

'Wherever there's a cardboard box I can call my own, and an empty lager can on which I can rest my weary head.'

Bassotti shook his head slowly and breathed: 'Fucking weirdo.'

'Just one last thing, Bert.' He was by the door now. 'What exactly are we dumping?'

Bassotti nodded and Tigger opened the sliding door at the back of the van, pushing it upwards to reveal a solid wall of black plastic refuse bags.

'Like I said, it's rubbish. OK, so it maybe is stuff you should take a bit more care of when you're getting rid of it. I know, these days, we should all think of the environment but sometimes you gotta cut corners. Any more problems?'

'Don't worry, Angel,' beamed Tigger, 'it's not nuclear.'

It wasn't household rubbish or kitchen waste either; there was no smell. Though that wasn't quite right. There was a faint, antiseptic whiff coming off the van.

Tigger read my mind: 'Paint, paint stripper, mild fungicides, the stuff decorators use. That's what you can smell, but don't worry, you won't get any on your clothes. I'm here to do all the heavy lifting.'

'Yeah,' said Bert, 'Tigger'll look after you.'

'That's what worries me,' I said to myself. 'OK, I'm in. Let me shift my wheels.'

Bassotti looked at me as if I had made an improper suggestion involving several members of his family.

'Well, you don't want an unattended black cab parked outside here for a couple of hours, do you?'

He considered this.

'Good thinking, Roy. Stick it round the corner, it'll be all right there.'

That was when I should have cut and run, just kept on driving leaving Bert and Tigger playing with themselves in the lock-up wondering what had happened to me. But the truth was it seemed easy money and I needed it. And a little bit of illegal dumping didn't seem so bad. I knew I might have to stay away from Greenpeace meetings for a while but they didn't issue death sentences just for fly-tipping, did they?

I drove Armstrong round the corner and parked under a streetlight; not that I relied on that to deter thievery but it was the sort of thing an honest civilian would do. There was little chance of Armstrong getting pinched. The young joyriders who went 'hotting' wanted something with a bit more speed, and the professional car thief would have a hell of a job selling him to anyone other than a real taxi driver and you can't imagine a real musher touching stolen property, can you?

In the glove compartment I found half a packet of Sweet Afton cigarettes I'd forgotten about, two pirate tapes of a Guns N' Roses studio session, a single black nylon stocking (which for the life of me I couldn't explain) and then, eventually, what I was looking for.

If you buy diesel at garages these days they have a dispenser near the pump which gives out cheap pairs of clear plastic gloves. I always take more than I need as, well, you never know.

I pulled on a couple of them – they are all one size and there is no 'left' and 'right' – and smoothed them down. They slipped and tore easily but at least they would do the job. I was damned if I was going to leave my fingerprints on Bassotti's van, if it was his, which I doubted.

It turned out to be the only sensible decision I made for quite a while.

3

So there we were, in the middle of one of the biggest, richest, most sophisticated cities in the world, at the start of the new decade of the Caring Nineties and we were taking a job, cash-in-hand, from a man we met in a pub.

Would you credit it?

It went off easy enough. Money for old rope, really. Well, old something or other.

We made it down the East India Dock Road before the pubs chucked out and then on to the A13, bypassing East Ham and Barking.

'We turn off here,' said Tigger unnecessarily. He hadn't said much during the trip, but I wasn't going to lose sleep over it. 'That's it, River Road. Now we hang a right just down here.'

I assumed he knew where he was going. As far as I could remember, though I didn't know the area well, River Road ran parallel to Barking Creek which eventually disgorged itself into the Thames. On the other side of the creek was a huge sewage works stretching almost as far as the Royal Albert Dock, which is light years away from the yuppified Docklands further upriver towards the City. Down here was real bandit country; or maybe that should be pirate country.

'There! Down there,' said Tigger, waving a hand in front of my nose. 'Right down there between those two warehouses.'

I swung the van over and flicked on the full beams of the headlights as we left the road on to a concrete wharf. The warehouses penned us in with their darkness and ahead the lights were beginning to waver and reflect off water.

In the distance, I could see the lights of the sewage works and my nose confirmed the sighting.

'Turn it round,' hissed Tigger, dropping his voice to a whisper. 'And kill the lights.'

I told him I didn't need telling to make sure I was pointing roughly in the Getaway direction, but unless we fancied a swim, I had no intention of killing the lights. Once pointed back towards the road, I turned off the ignition. We sat in silence for a few seconds. Somewhere in the distance a burglar alarm was ringing continuously, plaintively and unattended. Nothing unusual there.

Tigger had produced a pair of gardening gloves from the depths of his tracksuit and was pulling them on.

'You stay here, Roy. Have a smoke, abuse some substances, think dirty thoughts. You can leave the dirty work to me.'

'No doubts on that score, Tigger.'

He grinned at that and patted me on the knee again.

'I think I'm beginning to like you, Angel,' he said as he climbed out.

'Thanks for the warning,' I said to myself.

For ten minutes or so I watched him through the wing mirrors as he carted black plastic sacks from the back of the van and out of my sightline. At one point I thought I heard a splash, but I may have imagined it.

Then Tigger shut the doors with a bang and was back in the passenger seat, back in hyperactive mode, squirming around, pulling his gloves off and beating a riff with them on the plastic dashboard.

'Let's go go go go! It's payday and the night is young.'

'Then let's keep them in that order,' I said, holding out my hand, palm up.

Tigger gave my plastic glove a funny look, then shrugged as if to say each-to-his-own and began to unlace his right trainer, his foot up on the dash. When the shoe was off, he flipped it in the air and caught it with his left hand, then he put it on his right hand like a glove puppet and held it to his cheek.

'Hello, Hi-Top,' he mugged. 'Has pretty Hi-Top got some lovely folding stuff for Roy the Boy? He can only have it –

what? What was that, Hi-Top?' He put the shoe to his ear, like it was whispering to him. 'Only if he's very, very nice to you and gives you a kiss? Do you really mean that, Hi-Top? You want a kiss from rough old Roy?'

I sighed, turned all the van's lights on and leant on the horn.

'For fuck's sake!' yelled Tigger over the blast. 'OK, OK.'

His hand came out of the hi-top and it was holding five of the new twenty-pound notes. I took my hand off the horn and started the engine.

'Thank you, Mr Hi-Top.'

If Tigger had been silent on the way out to Creekmouth, he made up for it on the way back to the lock-up garage. He talked about how he was at a high risk point in his life and the more risks he took, the more he felt alive. But it was all cool because he'd read that the body was at its peak at his age and he could take it. At that he'd looked to see if he'd offended me but I didn't let it show that he had.

There was no sign of Bassotti at the lock-up and Tigger said he rarely stuck around. I asked how many jobs he'd done like this one and he said 'a few' and then asked me for a lift to King's Cross.

At that time of night, that meant one of two things and I didn't think he was going there undercover for the Salvation Army, but I said OK nonetheless. It had been implied as part of the deal and if there were more moonlight jaunts like this in the offing, I was in the market.

Across the City he sat on Armstrong's rumble seat and chatted away through the glass partition. He was going to experience everything he could before he was twenty-one, he said, and then he would make a decision on how he was to become famous. It might be music, it might be fashion. It would certainly be outrageous. Oh yes, the world was going to hear from Tigger O'Neil. And I shouldn't laugh (though I wasn't) because he was serious and was building up the cash reserves to break out.

'Break out of what?' I asked.

'The Talent Trap,' he said, dead straight. 'I don't have any natural talent except for showing off. That's what my school report always said: showing off. So, if you're gonna be a show-off, do it right, get professional help. That costs money. So I'm saving up. I don't have expensive habits, well, not that I pay for, and I live cheap and cheerful. The body can take it now, so store it all up as experience for the good life to come.'

As we hit a red light, I retrieved the pack of Sweet Afton from the glove compartment and lit up.

'You're weird,' I told him over my shoulder.

'And why's that, Mr Angel?' He reached through the partition and took the cigarette from my lips as I changed gear.

'Where are you from, Tigger?' I tried to change tack.

'From nowhere, going somewhere,' he said enigmatically, exhaling smoke into my ear.

I was right. He was weird.

As we approached King's Cross station, Tigger asked me to pull over near a letter box. I watched him in the mirror as he produced a brown envelope from his tracksuit and he checked the road both ways before he climbed out.

He wasn't worried about being mugged on the way to the letter box, he was watching the station concourse across the road and he took his time walking back to Armstrong.

'Change of plan,' he said as he got back in. 'Drop me at Lincoln's Inn, would you?'

'What's up? Is the scene too quiet for you?'

If he had been looking for the street-corner pick-up scene – which I doubted – he was in the wrong place anyway. All the kerb-crawling traffic was round the corner up York Way these days. There were too many lights at the entrance to the station and that discouraged passing trade. The huge entrance hall, however, still doubled as a meeting point for runaways and rent boys looking for a bed for the night, if only dossing down with some of the dopeheads and drunks too wrecked to care if they got taken in by the Transport Police or the Salvation Army. King's Cross wasn't as bad – or as popular, depending on your point of view – as some of the other mainline stations, but even at this time in the morning it seemed oddly quiet.

'There's been a Whittington,' said Tigger. 'I copped a view of the vans round the corner.'

The first police Operation Whittington, named after the legendary mayor of London, had concentrated on underground stations and had been designed as the human equivalent of an arms amnesty. The cops went round in groups of three, two uniforms and a woman constable, picking up anyone under eighteen who didn't look as if they had a home to go to. They were questioned, but not searched, and gently moved on: to a hostel or a night shelter if they wanted it, even back home if they could face it. Or just moved on, if they insisted. No arrests, no confiscations. What had surprised them, or more probably not the cops but the seriously liberal journalists who wrote it up, was the number of the younger homeless who happily refused the offer of sheltered accommodation. They had made their cardboard-box bed and they were going to lie in it.

'Lee will have gone by now,' Tigger said quietly. I asked who he meant.

'Lee. Just a friend. I do have friends, you know.'

'I'm surprised, I thought they might cramp your style.'

'Nothing, but nothing, cramps my style, Angel,' he said in tough guy mode.

Some tough guy.

I dropped him at Lincoln's Inn, outside a long-closed wine bar near the Old Curiosity Shop, and he got out of Armstrong on my side, standing next to the driver's door as if he wanted something. I let the window down.

'If you wanna do this again, I'd better have some way of contacting you.'

'Fair enough,' I agreed. 'I can give you a number.'

He went through a routine of patting himself down and then he smiled sheepishly to indicate no paper, no pen.

I dug a felt-tip out of my jacket and wrote the Stuart Street number on the inside of the top flap of the packet of Sweet Afton, the bit where they print 'The best that money can buy'. I was going to tear the flap off but he reached in and snatched the pack away from me.

'You really should quit, you know. Smoking's a young man's game.'

'So is getting a fat lip.'

He clutched both fists to his chin in mock terror, then put on his little-boy-lost look.

'You couldn't spare some change for a cup of tea, could you, guv'nor?'

'Come off it, Tigger, you got your wages tonight as well.'

'Honest, not a cent on me. Look.'

He pulled his tracksuit top up to his neck exposing a white hairless chest, then he twirled around in the middle of the road like a ballet dancer again and as he faced me his hands went to the waist band of the tracksuit bottom.

'Want to see everything?' he said loudly. 'Just to make sure?'

I took a pound coin from my pocket and flipped it at him and his hand snapped it up like a bird picking off an insect. He pulled the top down and shivered.

'Thank you, kind sir. It's getting too cold to go through the whole act.'

'It's a good act,' I said, putting Armstrong into gear. 'But where the hell are you going to get a cup of tea at this time of night?'

'Oh, I'm not. I just like to keep my hand in.'

We did two more runs that weekend on the same pattern. Tigger would ring me and arrange to meet in or near a pub in the East End. Bassotti would turn up looking uneasy and as if he had a better way of spending Friday and Saturday night. He probably had. I had; just couldn't afford it. Tigger almost certainly had, but that was probably illegal as well.

Bassotti would have one drink and then take Tigger in his car and I'd follow in Armstrong until we found a lock-up garage and a box van or a Transit already loaded to the roof with black plastic sacks. That made three different lock-ups and three different vehicles, but all in the general Bow or Mile End areas.

We used the same dumping ground down near Barking Creek on both occasions and both times Tigger did all the heavy lifting, insisting I stay in the van and keep look-out. And after dropping the van off, he'd got me to take him to King's Cross again and each time he stopped and used a letter box on the way. But what he did with his wages was his business.

The money was coming in useful, I have to admit. Hell, not just useful, vital. I stayed with the dispatch company but cut it to three days a week, which just about covered Armstrong's running costs.

To tell the truth, it kept me out of the house on Stuart Street which was becoming more depressing by the day.

Doogie and Miranda were having dry runs at packing all their worldlies into cardboard boxes, some of them so big they would have been classed as condominiums among Tigger's friends sleeping rough down at Lincoln's Inn. They still had over three months before Doogie moved north to coincide with one shooting season or other, but every day there would be a different combination of boxes and bags on the stairs. It was Miranda's way of deciding what could be shipped and what had to be sold. As they didn't have a car, they were trusting everything to either the postal system or the railways, so maybe they had a reason to be concerned. Yet the volume of sheer *stuff* which they seemed to have baffled me. When I'd arrived at Stuart Street, I had a Sainsbury's carrier bag. And I'd had trouble filling that.

Lisabeth and Fenella were no better. They had discovered iridology, staring deeply into each other's eyes and claiming to be able to diagnose not only present ailments, but past ones, by studying the iris of the eye. I did the old mine-look-like-road-maps routine ('you should see them from the inside') but they didn't see the funny side and went off in a sulk.

Even Springsteen kept out of the way, sensing my mood – or, more probably, my bank balance. Once the cans of cat food started to appear more regularly thanks to Bassotti's pay packets, then I saw him maybe twice a day for a snack, calling in from wherever he'd been to wherever he was going.

After the third trip, I didn't hear from Tigger for a couple of days and then an old mate called Bunny rang and asked if I fancied a few nights jamming at a club in the West End where they were trying to introduce Marengi music as the latest dance craze. I dusted off my faithful old B-flat trumpet, swilled water through it, spat out a couple of scales and made a mental note to buy some new lip-salve as the tube in the trumpet case could now double as sandpaper. Then I rang Bunny back and said sure, where and how much and, by the way, what the fuck was Marengi music anyway?

Marengi turned out to be the Dominican Republic's version of salsa, only less structured. That meant the brass section (Bunny on alto sax and me as two out of a seven-piece total) could do as much or as little as they liked and so could the dancers.

The club, off Oxford Street, was a flash place, but quality flash, no tat. The owner was an Iranian with money and no hang-ups about the Ayatollah, the Koran or the price of oil. He wandered around the club spreading bonhomie and free samples of Iranian caviar or triangles of toast in equal proportions. Halfway through the set he insisted the band tried some of his world famous collection of vodkas. I stuck with the lemon vodka but Bunny went straight in the deep end with the Bison-grass vodka followed by a Polish over-proof vodka which had been flavoured with brandy to tone it down. Almost immediately, the seven-piece band became a sextet but the dancers didn't seem to notice and Bunny didn't seem to care.

It was after two in the morning when I left carrying Bunny's saxophone case as well as my horn. Despite advanced numbness of most nerve endings brought on by the vodka-flavoured Bison (his words) he'd been drinking, he'd scored with a teenage brunette who said she was 'in publishing'. I didn't believe it as, for a start, her clothes smacked of so much money she obviously didn't have to work, and from her conversation, she had obviously never read a book in her life. Well, not one without pictures. Come to think of it, she could have been in publishing. Then again, she might have said she was in polishing. I wasn't paying much attention and I didn't really fancy her friend anyway.

One of the club's dinner-jacketed bouncers nodded to me as I left.

'You Angel?' he grunted, without moving his lips or unfolding his arms.

'I can get a message to him,' I said cheerfully. It's best to be reasonably honest with people like that.

'Friend of yours been waiting outside for an hour or so.'

He smirked the way doormen can get away with smirking.

Tigger was sitting on Armstrong's bonnet. He was wearing a baseball cap, T-shirt and jeans and was shivering. He rubbed his upper arms with his hands to keep warm.

'Bastards wouldn't let me in,' he said sulkily.

'Good. I'll put my name down for membership immediately. What are you doing here?'

'I rang you. Bassotti had a load on tonight but it's too late now. How about tomorrow? Meet at the Grapes again, in Rimmer Road?'

'When?' I asked suspiciously, remembering the 'Gay Karaoke Night' signs and the fact that tomorrow was Thursday.

'Closing time, out front?'

'Deal. How did you know I was here?'

'A real snotty bint answered your phone. Knew all about this gig and loved the sound of her own voice.' Fenella. She'd taken the original message from Bunny. I must have words with her one day.

'That your bit on the side, then?' Tigger pushed it as I dumped the instruments in the back of Armstrong. 'Or should that be your bit on the front as you heteros call it?'

I climbed into Armstrong and started him up. Tigger slid off the bonnet and tried the back passenger door.

'Hey! It's locked. I wanted a lift.'

He chased me out on to Oxford Street but the lights were with me and by the time I got to Oxford Circus he had vanished from my mirror.

*

The next night, he apologized before climbing into the back of Armstrong.

'Angel, I was well out of order last night.'

'That you were.'

From inside the pub came the amplified karaoke version of someone giving 'My Way' what for. Why was it always 'My Way' when it got to closing time?

'Is Tigger forgiven?' he came on, little-boy-lost.

'Some of us don't have all night, you know.' It was Bassotti, moving uncomfortably from one foot to the other beside his Sierra. He had the collar of his jacket turned up and even in the dark I could see his eyes blinking nervously. A neon sign flashing 'Drug Dealer' above his head might have made him look slightly less suspicious.

'Bert,' I acknowledged him and moved to kill the engine.

Bassotti dangled a set of keys in front of me.

'I can't hang about tonight. Tigger knows where the van is. Do the business and leave it where you found it. Flea-brain there can drop the keys off tomorrow.'

'If that's the way you want it.' I pocketed the keys.

From the back, Tigger was drumming on the rumble seat behind me with the palms of his hands, rapping: 'Let's go go go go, on the road with this show show show . . .'

Bassotti looked at him wearily and slowly shook his head.

'You can't get the staff these days,' I said, but if he found it funny he wasn't telling.

He turned and walked away, hands in pockets, but he didn't stop by the Sierra, he went diagonally across the car park. Ignoring the entrance to the pub, he disappeared behind a couple of parked cars, then I saw the glimmer of an interior light flick on and off and a door slammed.

'Go go go . . .' Tigger chanted from the back, but once we were out on the street, he stopped drumming and kneeled on the rumble seat so he could shout in my ear.

'The van's in Whitechapel, but there's no need for us to trek down to Creekmouth. I've found us a new dump site. Just the job. We can be done in five minutes and up West.'

'Does Bassotti know about this?'

'What he don't know can't aggravate his ulcers, can it?'

'Hey, I'm new on the payroll. Is it good policy to cross the boss this soon?'

'Relax. What makes you think he's the boss anyway? You'll get the same pay for ten per cent of the driving and I do all the heavy lifting again. Can you resist an offer like that?'

No. But I should have done.

4

The lock-up wasn't a lock-up this time. The white Transit van was simply parked at the side of one of the small streets off Stepney Way at the back of the old London Hospital in Whitechapel.

'Mile End Road as far as Stepney Green, then hang a left on to Globe Road.'

'Where are we going?' I asked, not trusting his sense of direction.

'It's called Globe Town,' Tigger said and I noted he was biting his lower lip.

'I know there's a place called Globe Town, but nobody goes there. You might go through it to get to somewhere else, but there's nothing there to stop for.'

'Exactly,' said Tigger.

He had done his homework, I had to give him that. He knew which side road to take once we had turned off Globe Road on to Roman Road, and which even smaller road to take off that. In fact, if Tigger hadn't been with me to point it out, I would have missed the entrance to the junkyard altogether.

'This is it. Go on, go in, it's OK.'

I had stopped to let the van's lights play on a pair of wide open double gates. One gate was resting off its hinges, the other bore the faded, hand-painted legend: HUBBARD'S YARD. I began to make out the pyramid shapes of piles of rusting car bodies organized in two lines; a scrap metal Valley of the Kings.

'Go on, then,' urged Tigger. 'Drive in and straight through.'

'Tigger,' I started patiently, 'this is somebody's yard, their place of business. Somebody works here, which means there are things worth nicking, which means they don't leave places like this undefended.'

'There's nobody here, I'm sure.'

'Then they'll have left a Doberman or a couple of pit bulls running around loose.'

'No dogs. No Dobermans, no pit bulls. Promise.'

'Not even an Alsatian with an attitude?'

'Not even a tomcat with an attitude.'

That didn't exactly inspire me with confidence, but he couldn't know why.

'Honest, I've sussed this place out. Anything worth having away is in the workshop and that's locked. Anyway, we're just driving through. Straight ahead and you come out on wasteland.'

'Down by the canal.' He looked surprised at that.

'You know where we are, then?'

'Roughly. We've just come through Bethnal Green and that' – I pointed to our right and up, where a stream of orange lights marked a last train heading for home – 'is the railway line into Liverpool Street and it goes over the Grand Union Canal somewhere round about here.'

'It took me days to find this place,' he said sullenly. 'But I have checked it out. Really. There's no one home.'

'OK, then,' I said, finding a gear, 'but just remember, I don't get out of the van.'

I moved the van into the yard less out of reassurance from Tigger than concern that even in a forgotten cul-de-sac, just sitting there with the engine running made us look suspicious.

There was a well-worn track between the two lines of heaped junked cars but I took it slowly, not wanting the Transit to hit a pothole or burst a tyre and end up adding to the accumulated dead weight of scrap. The effect of our lights hitting jagged edges of metal which had once been smooth and lovingly polished family pride-and-joy was weird. The cars were piled five or six high and the top ones leaned over at crazy angles. Most had doors and wheels missing. They were stacked as if on special offer on the shelves of a gigantic supermarket.

The avenue of wrecks ended to reveal waste ground sloping away in front of us and, to our left, a large windowless brick building with sliding doors big enough to admit a truck. They were firmly secured by three sets of hasps and padlocks on a scale which wouldn't have been out of place in the Disney version of *Jack and the Beanstalk*.

It was then that the floodlights came on and if I hadn't been busy trying to crash my way into reverse gear, I would have strangled Tigger.

'What's the matter?' he yelled at me as the gear stick screeched and began to fight back. 'Keep moving. You've just tripped the burglar lights, that's all.'

'That's all is it? Well, stroll bloody on. We're leaving.'

'They're just to frighten off the kids, they're not connected to an alarm or anything.' He had a hand on my hand on the gear stick. In some countries that meant marriage.

'And what about those, you airhead?'

I wrenched my hand free and pointed to the two remote video cameras now clearly visible above the sliding doors. They were not the moving sort which follow you around in high security buildings, but fixed to brackets on the wall. Each had a glowing red light just above the lens.

'Aw, come on, get real,' drawled Tigger. 'They're not even pointing this way. Look, Bassotti's got them all over his place. They cost nineteen pounds ninety-nine each, with batteries. They're fakes, man. They're just there for decoration, for fuck's sake. Relax will yer? The lights go off after a minute. Trust me.'

Trust me. Now those really should go down as classic Famous Last Words, along with 'Don't tell *me* how to change a fuse, woman'.

I found first gear and the van leapfrogged forward out of the glare of the floodlights and its own lights picked up a tower of rusting oil drums and more wrecks too far gone to be recognizable, with grass and weeds growing up between the skeletons of metal. We were bouncing now, over rough waste ground, the headlamp beams picking up tussocks of grass and small bushes. I swung the van in a slowing arc so I could turn and head back out. As we came round, the floodlights in the scrap yard went off and Tigger said: 'Told you so.'

I stopped the van but kept the engine running, as if that was what I'd intended to do all along.

'This do you?'

'Okey-dokey,' he chirped and climbed out after unclamping his hands from the dashboard where he'd hung on as I'd bounced us around.

I heard him open the rear doors and grunt as he hefted the first two bags. He was gone for about thirty seconds before he picked up the next. Over the sound of the engine I could only imagine I heard the occasional splash.

To my left, another train rattled out of Liverpool Street with only the odd passenger slumped in silhouette against the lit windows. In front of me, beyond the yard, a block of flats showed lights at almost every window. Any one of them could have offered a view of what we were doing.

Nobody was interested.

We left the van almost exactly where we had picked it up and Tigger pocketed the keys. Back in Armstrong, he cut me my wages and did the same trick he did every night, producing a folded envelope already stamped to put his share in.

'Where to? Lincoln's Inn again?' I asked.

'Not tonight, driver. Tonight we're going downmarket. Take me to the Strand.'

I started the engine and shook my head.

'You're not dooring it are you?'

'Variety is the spice of life,' he chirped.

'And the source of diseases,' I said.

Unlike Lincoln's Inn, where some of the tent dwellers had been there so long they received Reader's Digest mail shots, the area around the Strand and up into the Aldwych, was strictly transient. You were 'dooring' if you found an unoccupied doorway in which to fit yourself and your cardboard box or sleeping bag. The students at the London School of Economics called it 'their' cardboard city, but what do they know? They tried to organize a protest when the street-cleaning wagons came round at five a.m. to squirt the pavement and shop fronts with jets of icy water, but five a.m. is a pretty unrealistic time for a student. And in any case, the doorway population had moved out. Some went into Covent Garden and risked a night sheltering up against St Paul's church – the actors' church, used mostly for showbiz memorial services where actors lie through their teeth about other, dead, actors. Not that the church is a problem; it's a very nice church. It's just that it has been adopted by the most aggressive set of winos in London who regard any passing tourist as fair game for a bit of begging-with-menaces, and they didn't like newcomers on their patch.

Others would have cut up into Lincoln's Inn Fields and tried to crash the settlement there, either the permanent sites around the park railings where they have to chain their tents down and they use bright orange survival bags strung over the railings as windbreaks, or the no-man's-land in the middle around the folly, or pagoda, or whatever the hell it's supposed to be. They would only have done that if really desperate as the normal admission fee is a bottle. To defend their territory, the residents of the folly use old oranges, rescued from the backdoors of restaurants, tied in plastic carrier bags. They use them like demented gauchos throwing bolas and they hurt like stink when they hit. Look on the bright side. They haven't got guns. Yet.

The third migratory route would have been across the Hungerford footbridge to take their chance among the concrete of the South Bank. From there they could look over the river and see the mother of all Parliaments working late into the night. The government said there were less than a thousand people living rough on the streets of London. They also said the recession was over, inflation was coming down, beef was safe to eat and we had a Caring Society.

Whichever way the doorway people had gone, the exodus had not lasted long. Within a couple of months they were drifting back and cardboard boxes (especially from big electronic gear) were at a premium again.

'I suppose you want me to stop at a postbox,' I said.

'If you wouldn't mind, driver,' he answered, putting his

feet up on the glass partition behind my head. 'I'll have to be more careful. I'm getting set in my ways.'

Then I felt him looking at me as he said: 'Or maybe you're just more observant than most.'

I shrugged. 'So what's the big deal? You don't want to carry a roll of notes with you if you're going to be dooring it down the Strand, that stands to reason. So you post it to your Swiss bank account. None of my business.'

'You've never wondered about it? Go on, I'll say you have.'

'The only thing I've wondered about you, Tigger, is why you have to irritate people so much. It's not some breakaway Hare Krishna philosophy is it? Are you doing a degree in getting on people's tits?'

'Well, that's a reaction of sorts, I suppose,' he said cheerily. 'Most people I've done driving jobs with have decked me by the second one, or gone all high and mighty about my personal life.'

'You amaze me,' I said drily.

'Oh, Mr Angel,' he camped it up, putting his hands on his heart, 'I thought you didn't care. Worse still, I thought you hadn't noticed me.'

'That would be difficult, Tigger, though I'm sure there are drugs around these days that could help.'

'Why, Mr Cool, you can be so cutting. And you should be friends with Tigger, because Tigger will be famous one day.'

'Promise you won't forget the little people, won't you?'

I stopped near a postbox and watched him in the mirror again. He thought about something then got out, leaving Armstrong's door open so I couldn't drive off, posted his wages envelope and scurried back in.

'Home, James, to another night under the stars. And don't look so disapproving, Mr Angel. I can tell you are, even from here.'

'You're mistaking disapproval for total disinterest,' I said over my shoulder.

'Aw, come off it.'

He loomed in my mirror to take the drop-seat behind me. I felt his hand on my shoulder.

'We have a lot in common, you and me, Angel.'

I wondered if this was a come-on and, if it was, how I could best hurt his feelings without losing the driving job.

'Apart from a need for cash money and the oxygen in this cab, not a lot,' I said.

'Oh yes we do. Brothers in arms, that's what we are, bucking the system in our own different ways. Living life to the full.'

'Well you might be, but given the state of my finances, I'm living life to the tenth or thereabouts.'

'Stop moaning, you old tart! Admit it, if you were my age you'd be living the same life. We're both committedly irresponsible.'

'No we're not. Well, I'm not,' I argued.

'Oh, my mistake,' he trilled. 'I'd forgotten about the house and two-point-four kids out in the suburbs, and the day job, and the mortgage and this must be the company's Ford Escort I'm riding in. Get real.'

'What is this, Tigger? You going in for psychiatry at night school or something? Get a life, but not mine.'

He laughed.

'See, exactly my point. You're a professional sidestepper, just like me except you even sidestep admitting it to yourself.'

'Was there a special sort of glue on that envelope you posted back there, or is it a full moon tonight?'

'Cheap shot, Angel. I've thought about this and to be really free, you can't afford to be responsible for anyone or anything. The minute you start to give a shit about what you do or what people think of you, you're no longer a free agent.'

'Must be a rough life,' I said.

And a short one; as it turned out.

The weekend at Stuart Street crawled by in a succession of futile arguments with Lisabeth and Fenella and only a minor piece of sabotage to the plans of Doogie and Miranda.

Doogie's move back to Scotland had been prompted by the offer of a job as top chef in a posh hotel-cum-leisure complex on the banks of some loch or other. The actual location was a historic Scottish family house, fortified against the natural

45

elements, the English, the Scots, and the Scots who always fought for the English (like the Armstrongs). It had survived those four apocalyptic horsemen only to fall to the fifth: tourism.

For Doogie, it was a plum job. It offered a limited working season, lots of under-chefs under him and he could vote Scots Nationalist at the election without having to spoil his ballot paper as he did in Hackney.

All I had done was point out to Miranda that it would be difficult for her to continue her career in local journalism up there owing (a) to the lack of newspapers, and (b) the illiteracy rate among Highland cattle. She had thought about this and, for a moment, seemed to be putting a brave face on things. Then I suggested – just suggested, mind – that there would always be lots of openings for staff in a new hotel-cum-leisure complex, such as waitresses, chambermaids, kitchen staff even. And you couldn't have a more understanding boss than Doogie, could you?

It was at this point she decided Doogie ought to stay in on Saturday night so they could have a 'relationship assessment'. I don't know how it went, and I didn't like to pry, but Doogie didn't speak to me for three days and even then I don't suppose you could call 'Turn the fookin' music down!' yelled down the stairs, polite social conversation.

By Sunday evening, Lisabeth and Fenella weren't talking either. Well, certainly not to me and probably not to each other.

They were still plotting a move to Glastonbury as a centre of ley lines and the earth's sacred and spiritual linear forces. Lisabeth had found a book in the local library which seemed to substantiate this theory by referring to *Feng-shui*, one of the ancient Chinese beliefs similar to the basic philosophical principle of Taoism, which regards the earth as a living thing through which life-force flows on 'dragon paths'. The *Feng-shui* practitioner would build his house or tomb along these flow lines to ensure the best vibes, just like an acupuncturist knew exactly which flow line to tap with his needles.

I upset them first by reminding them that their last experiment with acupuncture had cost them a fortune in Elastoplasts. Then I pretended to understand what they were on about and conned them into wasting Saturday morning in the library looking through guide books trying to find pubs called the Green Dragon which would be good pubs because they were bound to have been sited on ley lines.

While they were out, I left a message near the communal wall phone telling them to ring the number of the nearest Chinese take-away as their *Feng-shui* was ready and did they want noodles or plain rice?

I even managed to give the mysterious Mr Goodson the hump, though I didn't intend to.

Mr Goodson keeps himself to himself, doesn't drink, smoke or indulge in illegal substances and doesn't play loud music. In all other respects, he's a perfect house-mate. We rarely see him during the week and never at weekends, so maybe I over-reacted when I saw him letting himself out of the front door as I emerged on the Sunday morning to collect my milk.

It was still some ungodly hour, say about ten o'clock, and I hadn't expected to meet anyone on the stairs so I was wearing just a towel scooped up off the bathroom floor, and to be honest, was still half asleep. So when I yelled a cheerful, neighbourly greeting, it actually came out as: 'Good son, Mr Morning.'

He gurgled something from the back of his throat, nodded in my general direction and hurried out the door. He was wearing a knee-length duffel coat of the sort you only see these days on historical newsreels of Ban the Bomb marches – and you only see them when a socialist politician or arch-bishop snuffs it. He was carrying a huge sports bag over his shoulder and though it said CICA in big letters, it didn't fool me into thinking he was off to do something athletic. Maybe he was doing a moonlight flit or just deserting the sinking ship like everybody else seemed to be.

If he was I wondered how long it would be before anyone noticed.

Monday morning involved two big decisions. The first was whether to hide in the bathroom until our esteemed landlord

Nassim Nassim had been and gone, thus avoiding paying the rent. Again.

Given the mood of the rest of the house, any one of them was likely to grass me to Nassim so I bit the bullet and clocked on with the dispatch company. By seven o'clock I was on Baker Street again, facing big decision two: whether to hang around Porter Street and use the McDonald's or defect across the street to the Burger King which had put out tables and benches to try and win back trade. As Tony, the Beast from the East, was already sprawled out on one of the benches, that made it easy; I would wait until he wasn't looking, then nip into McDonald's.

Before I could, the radio squawked.

'Oscar Seven, Oscar Seven. You out there?'

I started Armstrong's engine again before answering.

'Oscar Seven. Am in West One, heavy traffic.'

The only thing moving on Baker Street was a Vulture refuse truck, its great iron jaws at the back gobbling up the black plastic sacks as the bin men hurled them in with unfailing accuracy.

'Special request for you, Oscar Seven. Cash customer specified black cab for two passengers, West One area, soon as you can.'

It was too early in the day to tell if this was a wind-up or not, but some of the guys on Dispatch can get really warped after a quiet night on the switchboard.

'Pick up and destination?'

'Seymour Street, outside Barclays Bank.'

'And where to, Dispatch?'

'Passenger's name is O'Neil. Cash not account. ETA?'

They never tell you the destination, in case you pick up a better fare – like an airport – en route, so you always feel a right wally having to ask the customer: 'Where to?'

'Five minutes,' I said, knowing they'd say ten.

I thought no more about it than the fare might just pay for the diesel I'd used already that morning. I didn't connect 'O'Neil' with anything and didn't bother asking for more details, just blithely assumed that there wouldn't be too

48

many people hanging around outside a bank at that time of the morning.

There weren't. Just one. Tigger.

He was hopping from foot to foot, more agitated than usual and when he saw me coming he waved frantically.

I slowed at the kerb and leaned over and pulled the window down.

'Don't fuck about, Tigger, I'm working.'

'I know you are, I called you,' he said breathlessly, opening the back door.

I slid back the driver's partition as he climbed in. His tracksuit top was soaking wet down the chest and he reeked badly of vomit. Before I could order him out or kill the engine, he waved a bunch of ten-pound notes at me.

'Genuine, Angel, straight-up hire. Look, I've got the dosh, now drive.'

'Where to, sir?' I said, like the dispatch company had taught me.

'Down here.' He pointed to Seymour Place. 'We're picking somebody up. I'll show you. Then Lincoln's Inn. Look, I told you, I've got money.'

'Where did you get it?' I asked as if it was any of my business.

'I've been to the bank. Hole-in-the-wall job. Cash available twenty-four hours. Now will you sodding well drive?'

I picked up the crappy radio they'd rented me and called it in: POB – passenger on board – to Lincoln's Inn. Dispatch feigned interest, saying they could maybe find me something in Holborn by the time I got there.

I swung into Seymour Place and put my foot down, mildly curious as to why Tigger was lying to me.

5

If I'd had reservations about Tigger getting in the cab, it was going to take an advance course of sensory deprivation to persuade me to let his friend join him in the back of Armstrong.

We hadn't gone far, just down Seymour Place and then hanging a right before Marylebone Road into one of the small streets at the back of the Marylebone branch of Westminster Library. At this time of the morning it was notorious as a dossing area for the sad old winos wearing three jackets and someone else's trainers who had been moved along – or more accurately, moved out – from Baker Street underground station or the nearby subway which stank of urine worse than any urinal.

And that was exactly what I thought we'd got to begin with.

Tigger made me stop and was out of Armstrong before I could complain. When I saw him bending over the figure slumped against the wall of a discreet, but high priced, estate agent's ('Flats from £490 per week'), I left the engine idling and got out. My only thought was to close the back door and get out of there, but then Tigger saw the look on my face.

'Come on, Angel, you've got to help,' he said in what I guessed was his normal voice. 'I'm paying you, remember.'

'Means nothing,' I said, looking at the figure on the pavement. There was no blood immediately in evidence, that was something, but whoever it was had decided he liked his breakfast so much he had wanted to see it again. Close up. On his T-shirt.

'I've got money,' snapped Tigger.

He reached into a trouser pocket and produced another wedge of notes, all seemingly twenty-pound ones, folded in half and obviously old.

'From the bank, you said,' I said vaguely.

Tigger wasn't looking at me. He was trying to put an arm around the vagrant's shoulder. Needing both hands, he pushed the notes back into a pocket.

'What?'

'Let it ride.'

It suddenly didn't seem important to ask Tigger where he'd got the money. Notes like that would never have come out of a hole-in-the-wall cash machine, even if there had been one at the bank Tigger said he'd been to.

The reason I stopped worrying about it was that I got my first good look at the corpse Tigger was trying to resurrect. It wasn't a corpse, of course, it was a kid – a skinny blond boy who could pass for eighteen in a dimly lit pub and maybe fool the Social Security that he was sixteen, but was probably nearer thirteen. Along with his vomit-stained T-shirt he wore a pair of black ski pants, but no shoes. The black footstraps were indistinguishable from the filthy soles of his feet. I looked back to his face as Tigger tried to raise his head again.

'Come on, Lee, it's OK, you're down now,' he was saying. The kid's head snapped back, a lock of blond hair stuck to one cheek with snot or vomit or saliva. He didn't seem to have any eyeballs, or none that faced outwards anyway.

'What's he on?' I asked, not wanting to know because it would mean I would be involved.

'He's been to a party,' said Tigger, still trying to get the kid upright. 'These aren't his clothes. It was that sort of party.'

'I didn't ask about his dress sense or his social life.'

'I think he's been smoking Amp,' said Tigger quietly.

'Oh shit.'

'I think he's broken his hand, but he doesn't know it yet.'

He moved to one side so I could see the kid's right hand. At first guess I would have said a Number 159 bus had run over it. Possibly a 73. That was why Tigger had crouched the way he had, shielding the crushed hand which was red with blood and black with dirt. The dirt you could clean, but no one touches blood these days.

'Probably did it when he landed,' I offered.

Tigger nodded and just breathed.

'Yeah.'

'Amp', believe it or not, is good old marijuana – that quaint social drug from those innocent days when people smoked and wore fur – soaked in embalming fluid. Now who thought that one up?

The effects of smoking it (and it's easier to buy than cigarette tobacco on some railway stations) were similar to that of the drug PEP, which the Americans called 'Angel Dust'. In the early Eighties, there had been numerous cases of Angel Dusters trying to take on the rush hour traffic in the middle of the Los Angeles freeway system. I had once met a paramedic with the LA Fire Department who had seen Viet Nam, the Watts riots and gone into blazing buildings without turning a hair, who dreaded attending a call out to an Angel Duster.

'Where did he get it?'

'Does it matter?'

'No, I suppose not.'

Somewhere, a couple of streets away, a burglar alarm went off. It was nothing to do with us and under normal circumstances, we would have put it down to the white noise of London's street life. At that time of day it was invariably going to be either an employee arriving early at a shop or a cleaner leaving an office without thinking. But the noise galvanized us into action.

'You wanted to go to Lincoln's Inn Fields, right?'

'Yeah,' said Tigger, looking all the time at Lee's boyish face, not at me. 'There's a medic, a lady doctor, comes round first thing in a morning, just to check on us – them.'

'Then let's go. The meter's running, so to speak. Waiting time's extra.'

Minicabs, which Armstrong now pretended to be, don't have meters just rates per mile and any extra waiting time usually came out as the driver's tip.

Tigger nodded gratefully but still did not move. Down the

street, a couple of women on their way to work crossed to the other side of the road to avoid walking near us.

'Come on, Tigger, let's roll.'

'I can't lift him by myself,' he said, his voice cracking.

I bit my lower lip, then opened Armstrong's door and reached into the glove compartment for a pair of the plastic gloves I'd used before when we were in the van.

I pulled them on and took Lee by his left arm and leg, leaving Tigger to handle the damaged side, and we bundled him into the back of the cab.

Tigger sat with Lee's head in his lap and didn't say a word all the way over to Lincoln's Inn. I made a mental note to remind myself to burn the gloves as soon as I got the chance, and to steal another three pairs from the garage the next time I filled up with diesel.

It pays to think ahead.

Despite its resident population, Lincoln's Inn Fields still remains a regular pit-stop for real black cabs and real cabbies. You can find up to twenty parked along the east side of the Fields at certain times of day, near the public toilets which, surprisingly, given the resident squatters, are in pretty good shape. It is sufficiently off the beaten track to enable a professional musher to have ten minutes with a newspaper, a sandwich or just a quick kip, without being pestered by potential fares or, even worse, tourists wanting directions but not a cab ride.

I turned Armstrong into the Fields from Holborn and pulled up, not wanting to go round the square and mix with the professionals. They didn't like delicensed black cabs being run by anyone in London, and certainly not operated as minicabs.

'Where's this medic, then?' I asked Tigger over my shoulder.

'She should be . . . there . . . over there by the camouflage basha.'

I spotted what he meant. Someone had used Army camouflage netting, two poles and two branches of a plane tree to construct a three-sided tent with a sagging roof. Outside it stood a tall, thin woman in a white surgical coat. She seemed to be negotiating with the inhabitant of the basha and not at all keen to bend down and crawl inside.

I turned back to Tigger.

'Can he walk?'

'I doubt it,' he said. 'But he's breathing more confidently.'

Oh great. We faced the prospect of carrying him between us like some safari kill. As if Tigger couldn't draw enough attention to himself normally.

'What's the medic called?' I tried.

'Doc,' said Tigger. Then: 'Where are you going?'

'To see if she makes house calls.'

She did, or at least she thought it perfectly natural to treat a comatose young druggie with a broken hand in the back of a taxi at the side of the road as the civilians wandered by to their office jobs.

'Doc' had spine-length hair twisted tight into a pony tail and segmented every three inches or so by a coloured rubber band. As she bent over to look at Lee in the back of Armstrong, I could see that her designer-label jeans fitted her well, with no visible panty line.

In an accent which I later found out was Canadian, she gave me instructions to drive to what she called a safe house on Gray's Inn Road, close to the hospital. There were no prizes for guessing it was a medics' house – students and junior doctors – who ran a vigilante rescue service for druggies and drop-outs. I'd heard of a similar operation up at the university teaching hospital which ran a helpline for sexually transmitted diseases.

On the way there, she asked Tigger a battery of questions about Lee's health, diet and lifestyle, though she never asked his name. Once there, she jumped out of Armstrong and ran to the voice-access bell push.

She said something and headed back. Within a minute, two other females had opened the door and joined us.

Between them, they bundled Lee into the house without asking for help from either Tigger or me.

'Hey, Doc,' I shouted, but not too loudly, 'will he be able to play the violin when you've finished with him?'

'Sure he will,' she said, giving me a smile.

'That is fucking amazing, Doc, 'cos he couldn't play a note up till now.'

It got a laugh and broke the tension. Even Tigger smiled nervously.

'I'd better stay and see he's OK,' he said. 'How much do I owe you?'

'Make it twenty quid,' I said, bumping the mileage rate.

Tigger handed over two twenty-pound notes without blinking and stood in front of me weighing up the rest of his roll of notes.

'I'd better make a donation or something,' he said vaguely. 'Doc looks after us, you know.'

'She's very impressive,' I offered, realizing how difficult it was to fold money while wearing plastic gloves.

'Never preaches, never grasses.'

'A real saint. See you around.'

'Yeah. I'll be in touch. Owe you one.'

He pointed a finger at me like a gun then skipped up the stairs and into the safe house.

On the Thursday, Tigger rang and arranged a meet for the Friday night for another little driving job. I agreed to meet him at eleven-thirty in Lambeth, near the hospital and the Elephant and Castle tube station.

The mention of a hospital prompted me to ask after Lee, but Tigger seemed vague and uninterested, dismissing me with: 'Yeah, yeah, he's fine. See you tomorrow and don't hang about.'

He was no more forthcoming the next night. I watched him walk, jog and hop through the streetlight towards Armstrong and put it down to his normal hyperactive self. His natural mode of movement seemed to be based on a Michael Jackson video played backwards.

'You can leave the cab here,' he said through my window; 'the van's round the corner.'

'Hi, there, Tigger, good to see you,' I said sarcastically. 'How's Lee?'

'He's going to be all right,' Tigger replied without looking at me. 'I'm going to look after him. Come on, we've got to get this shit over to Globe Town.'

'What? Back over the river?' I fell into step beside him, although Tigger would never be able to say 'Walk this way' as no one else could.

'Yes. Same place as last time.'

'Why? Isn't there anywhere around here we can dump it?'

He held out a set of keys as we turned a corner. Twenty yards away was a parked white Transit van.

'It's got to be Globe Town and I'll make it worth your while because this could be the last run.'

'How worth my while?' I asked, pulling on the pair of leather gloves I'd remembered to bring.

'Double.'

'OK. I can be bought.'

I slowed down as we turned off Roman Road and approached the junkyard.

'Just go in the yard and turn round this time,' Tigger said quietly.

'What's up?' I was instantly nervous and ready to hit reverse. 'Does the alarm system work all of a sudden?'

'No, nothing like that, I've just found a better place. Trust me, Angel. Stay in here and let me do the dirty work. Keep the engine running if you want. Trust me, there's nobody here.'

I eased the van through the half-open gate advertising Hubbard's Yard and swung it round in a circle, killing the lights in the process. I left the engine ticking over.

'I won't be long,' said Tigger, slithering across the seat.

He was wearing a shell suit with purple and orange stripes. It looked like the sort of garment they give you after they've taken away your real clothes and sharp objects and put you in the cell next door to that nice Dr Lecter.

He turned as he opened his door, but I held up a hand to forestall him.

'If you say "Trust me" one more time, I'm phoning the Samaritans.'

'Give 'em my love,' he grinned, jumping out.

'Yeah, I reckoned you'd have an account with them,' I said to myself.

I switched off the engine and took the keys from the ignition. I had wound down my window by the time Tigger appeared sheepishly with his hand out.

'Er . . . the back doors are locked.' He saw the dangling keys. 'Thanks.'

'Want a hand, to speed things up?' I offered.

'No.' He said it quickly; too quickly. 'I can manage. Don't get out.'

I stayed in the cab, my fingers twitching on the wheel until he had opened the back doors and brought back the keys. Knowing I could at least drive away calmed me down a bit, but not enough. In the wing mirrors I could see Tigger taking two black plastic bags on a trip to somewhere in the darkness of the yard and once I heard a screech of metal and a crash, followed by a distinct 'Shite!' as something gave way under him.

He made three trips in all; six bags. Then he appeared at my window again.

'Got a pen on you?'

'As a matter of fact, yes,' I said, startled, but handing over a black felt-tip.

'Don't ask,' he said and winked.

He disappeared back into the yard and was gone for three or four minutes before reappearing in the nearside mirror. As he walked towards the passenger door, I could see him tucking an envelope into the waistband of his trousers. 'That's it, we're out of here,' he said, piling in.

'You said something about double the wages.' I held out a hand. 'I hope that doesn't mean I have to ask you twice.'

He sighed and tore open a velcro pocket. 'Oh ye of little faith,' he said, handing over a fold of notes.

'That way I'm rarely disappointed.'

Tigger held up his right hand as if he was administering a blessing.

'I abjure thee, vile spirit and by expelling thee, heal all wounds.'

I started the Transit's engine.

'Don't throw a wobbler on me now, Tigger. Wait till we're south of the river.'

'No wobblers.' He drummed a riff on the dashboard. 'Job's done, time to take a break. I'm going to have a monster weekend.'

'Good for you.' I was concentrating on my mirror looking for rogue police cars or some of the local tribesmen. It wasn't a good area to be cruising after midnight. Even the pit bulls went round in pairs.

'You can drop me at the Ritz,' Tigger said dreamily.

'Sure.' I let him see me eyeing his shell suit. 'Formal dress tonight, is it?'

'Now, now, you old tart, don't knock it till you've tried it.'

I checked the rearview again and reckoned we were free and clear.

'I know I'm going to regret this, but tried what?'

'The Friday night throw-outs from the kitchens. Once the rich people have gone, the street people get to lick the plates.'

'Tigger, you've just given me two hundred notes, so somewhere about your unwashed little person, you've got at least the same if not more. You can afford a square meal, for Christ's sake.'

'That's not the point, Angel. You get to meet some interesting street people. Lots of kids from up north, middle-class runaways, druggies, winos – all human lowlife is there. And then, of course, there are the rich punters looking to pick up a bit of lowlife to satisfy their appetites.'

I said nothing.

'They're the best of all, because they know they have to pay for their pleasure. Even if it's not cash on the spot, they pay eventually. And they know they have to, that's the beauty of it. They feel so guilty about their appetites . . .'

'Tigger, I really don't want to know this,' I sighed.

'That's what it's all about, Angel. Appetites. Satisfy your appetites as soon as you can. Find out what you like, have your fill, then move on. If you don't, you'll miss out and regret it forever, or you'll try later in life and your appetites will betray you.'

'Tigger, that's bullshit.'

'Well, excuse me, Mr Conformity. Pardon me if my lifestyle offends but from where I'm sitting, the only thing that's different between us is that I'm still young enough to be taking my chances and enjoying them.'

I checked the mirrors again and dropped down a gear.

'There are other differences. Important ones.'

'Such as?' he sneered.

'Like I'm the one driving, and you're not wearing a seat belt.'

We left the van roughly where we'd picked it up and reclaimed Armstrong.

Tigger still wanted to go to the Ritz even though Big Ben showed it was two a.m. as we recrossed the river.

I dropped him on Piccadilly near Green Park tube station.

'I can't tempt you, then?' he beamed as he climbed out of Armstrong on the driver's side.

'No way.'

I should have said 'Take care' or something similar but I didn't. Over towards Berkeley Square, a car alarm went off and when I looked again, Piccadilly was empty and Tigger had disappeared.

6

'Angel?'

'Yeah?'

'Are you still busy?' Fenella's pleading was getting close to a whine by now.

'You know I'm busy every Sunday afternoon, Fenella.' In this case, reading a second-hand Sunday newspaper someone had left down the pub at lunch time.

'I've finished the washing up,' she said from the doorway of the kitchenette. 'And I've cleaned all the surfaces and decrusted Springsteen's dish.'

That was odd. I hadn't heard her using a flame-thrower.

'If you move the meat, I'll clean out the fridge for you.'

She was desperate and I couldn't stand it any more.

'OK,' I said, folding the newspaper and taking my socks off the coffee table, 'what do you want?'

'Just some advice, really.'

She came into the room and sat primly on the chair farthest from me.

'OK, the doctor is in and the meter running. Tell me where it hurts.'

She looked at me blankly, shook her head slightly and took a deep breath.

'Do you need a licence to drive a caravan?'

It was my turn to ring up the 'Vacant' sign.

'Er . . . you mean a camper?'

'No, a caravan, a proper caravan. You know, a gypsy caravan – a Romany caravan – sort of upside-down horseshoe shape with a chimney with a triangle on top and a split door you can lean over and –'

'Little wooden steps at the back,' I offered without enthusiasm.

'That's it!' she squealed. 'And my . . . a little pony to pull it, with a long mane and white socks, which we could ride at the weekends.'

'You and Lisabeth, huh?'

She nodded, her face flushed.

'You're gonna need a bigger horse. Maybe a Shire or a Suffolk Punch.' Her face said she ought to be taking this in, maybe making notes.

'This is your latest, is it? Going native and joining the New Age travellers in the West Country.'

'That's right, we need a change of life, not just lifestyle.'

I wondered where she'd read that.

'I never knew you were into drugs and trespassing and scrounging social security hand-outs. I would have said that went against everything the Binkworthy family stood for.'

Fenella stood up and stamped a foot. I hoped it wasn't a signal to Lisabeth in the flat below.

'Mr Angel, you are the last person I would have expected to hear that from. Just because the newspapers say things like that doesn't mean it's true. I'm talking about free spirits who can't and won't be tied down by an uncaring, materialistic society. I thought you would have understood.'

'OK, calm down. Does Lisabeth know about this?'

'No, not yet.' She sat down again and licked her fingers before rubbing cat hair off her trousers. 'It was going to be a surprise.'

Knowing Lisabeth's aversion to Springsteen, the idea of her living with anything bigger, especially something which could produce manure on a commercial scale, would certainly be a surprise.

'You're really set on moving out, aren't you?'

'Yes, we are. London is bad for the inner self. Doogie and Miranda are moving north, we're going west.'

'Doogie's going to work for some rich capitalists in Scotland and will probably start a salmon rustling business on the side. There's a difference.'

'Well, we're set on it because we want to find ourselves before the millennium.'

She fingered something hanging around her throat. It looked like a velvet spell-pouch but knowing how sensitive her skin was, it probably contained dried parsley or basil from Sainsbury's.

'Fine, whatever you say. I'm convinced I'm going to be the only one left in London throwing a New Year's Eve party in 1999.'

'That won't worry us,' Fenella said primly. 'Lisabeth hates parties.'

'I didn't know she liked horses.'

'She will, she's just not experienced them before.'

Nor they her.

'Then you're on your own, kid, but I think you do need a licence,' I lied, neither knowing nor caring if you did or not.

'You mean a driving test?'

'That's the way most people get them. But if you get one, you might as well get a car or a van or a camper. That might go down better with Lisabeth.'

Her face brightened at that.

'You're right. She'd like it if I could drive her around.' Then came the frown. 'But you have to have lessons, don't you?'

'Lots.'

She thought about this.

'Would you teach me?'

'Er . . . I . . . it's never . . .'

'I'd pay. Whatever the going rate is.'

Was I that desperate?

'I don't know what the hourly rate is, but I'll find out – leave that to me.'

'And Lisabeth mustn't know,' she whispered.

'That could be difficult and I don't know how I could deceive her like that. It wouldn't be right.' It was my turn to act the primp.

Fenella's eyes lit up with an idea.

'If you wanted things doing round the flat, you know, the

washing-up and cleaning and things, I'd help out when she wasn't around.'

'Let me think about it,' I said trying to figure out where to get a car. There was no way I was trusting her with Armstrong.

'I won't do baths, though.'

'What?' I said vaguely, trying to work out how long I could spin this out.

'I don't like cleaning out baths.'

'Oh, don't worry about the bath,' I said dismissively. 'That doesn't need cleaning, it has water in it nearly every day.'

I ducked as she flung a cushion at my head.

''Ere, Angel, are you Oscar Seven?'

I looked up from the crossword of a *Daily Telegraph* which my one and only job of the morning had left in the back of Armstrong.

'You know I am, we work for the same company.'

The Beast from the East creaked his leathers as he levered off the top of his carton of coffee. He had been sitting opposite me in the Baker Street McDonald's for a good five minutes (or the time taken to ingest two Egg McMuffins, whichever is longer) before speaking. I had only nodded when he sat down because I was busy filling in the answer to three down – 'primitive' – which had just come to me in a flash.

'Yer, well, they were after you on the radio.'

I waited. And waited. Could the answer to eight across really be 'dickhead'?

'When was this exactly?'

'As I was parking the bike,' he said.

Next to your brain, but I didn't say it.

'Got your radio with you?'

'Nope.'

'Thanks. Finish that for me.' I pushed the crossword at him and stood up.

Armstrong was parked around the corner on Porter Street, opposite the London office of the Fulbright Commission. I gave their front door a longing look and wondered if they took charity cases straight off the street.

I thumped the tinny Korean radio and called in to Dispatch.

'My God, Oscar Seven's alive and answering. Wonders never cease.'

'Yeah, yeah, yeah. Got anything for me?'

'A *personal* request,' said Dispatch as if it hurt him. 'Job out at Stratford.'

'Stratford? That's on my doorstep. I could have stayed in bed this morning.'

'From your response time, I thought you had.'

'Oh, very quick. Not funny, but very quick.'

'Count your blessings, Oscar Seven. The customer is willing to wait. Specific request for Roy in the black cab to do a few deliveries around the East End. I offered any amount of better drivers but he insisted on you.'

'Who did?'

'Very insistent he was. Only Roy in the black cab would do.'

'Who? Where? Who asked for Roy?'

'Said he thought your call sign might be "Angel" but I said we wouldn't have such a daft call sign over the airwaves . . .'

'Look, do I get an address or do I have to wait for the next eclipse?'

'Didn't I mention it? H.B. Builders, Navigation Road Industrial Estate, Stratford Marsh. Ask for a Mr Bert. That's B for Bastard, E for Erection, R for Rectum and T for . . .'

'Tosser,' I said helpfully.

Of course, it was Bert, as in Umberto. That nice Mr Bassotti, who was probably the 'B' in H.B. Builders, who gave total strangers envelopes of money to fly-tip rubbish across our fair capital city because the reformed, privatized local councils didn't want to know or charged for the honour of taking it away.

As I threaded my way eastwards to Stratford Marsh, I thought the special request for me meant another *Wages of Fear* job driving dangerous – well, certainly dodgy – cargoes across the badlands. In *Wages of Fear*, though, it was nitro-glycerine falling off the back of the lorry. Tigger and I had been carrying nothing more dangerous than . . . whatever it had been we were carrying. Paint. It had probably been old paint cans, I told myself. They had been fairly light as Tigger had carried two sacks at a time on some occasions. And empty paint cans were a bugger to get rid of, weren't they? Probably old stock and with a higher than permitted level of lead.

Something like that.

Yeah, I decided, it had been old paint cans, maybe even nicked paint originally. I remembered working a summer in a small fishing village near Youghal in County Cork and the local fish cannery treated itself to a new light blue paint job, all good weather-resistant, quality stuff. By the end of August every fishing boat for five harbours up the coast was light blue all of a sudden.

That sort of thing always happens and builders use a lot of paint. Then again, builders dig a lot of holes and holes are good places to drop rubbish in. But where was the percentage in worrying? Unless we had actually been spreading toxic or nuclear waste, my conscience would handle it; once I got around to asking it.

As I turned Armstrong into Navigation Road, I saw the sign for H.B. Builders leading into a yard.

Most small time building contractors tend to be Something & Son, even though it rarely lasts a full generation. I would have thought Bassotti & Sons would have been more popular given his Italian roots, though he had been pretty lukewarm about them when I'd first met him in the pub. He must be the only Italian male in London not pleased to have Italian League soccer on TV now.

Or maybe he was being practical, thinking who would trust an Italian builder. All the potential jokes about leanings in Pisa and the Colosseum not being finished yet would be enough to piss off anyone. Maybe the 'H' in H.B. stood for 'Hubert to distance his Italian name even further. Maybe he didn't have any sons. Maybe I should stop talking to myself.

The first person I saw as I bounced Armstrong into the yard was Bassotti and he looked as out of place there as he had in the bar of the Grapes.

He was standing straddle-legged across a rut of mud shouting instructions to the driver of a JCB mechanical digger. The JCB driver kept revving the engine and inching forward, sending up a fine spray which Bassotti was unaware of, the hem of his £450 grey-green Jaeger overcoat gradually turning brown.

Even from inside Armstrong I could see that the weasel-faced driver was taking the rise out of Mr B., as he nodded and kept saying 'Yes, yes, right away' and all the time blinking rapidly. Bassotti seemed unaware of the imitation, or maybe he was used to it.

He noticed me and held out a hand, palm up like a cop, then waved me over to the other side of the yard. He held up one finger, pointed it at me and then pointed to a prefabricated site office ten yards away. Just in case I got lost, the words SITE OFFICE had been stencilled on the hardboard door.

As I parked Armstrong, I watched in the mirror as the JCB driver leaned out of his cab and blinked Bassotti straight in the eyes. Then he nodded in the universal 'Sure, sure, 'course I'll do it' way and pulled away. Bassotti turned, picking his footsteps carefully, and walked towards the office. Weasel-features in the cab of the JCB stuck a hand out and gave the finger gesture to Bassotti's back.

The yard was splattered with builder's junk. There were two piles of old bricks which needed cleaning up and pallets of new ones which were only worth half as much as the 'seconds' which were what the trendy home-improver went for. Similarly there were piles of old roofing tiles which were worth more in Hampstead than the houses they had once roofed in Shoreditch. There were two small flat-back lorries with 'H.B. Builders' on the front in faded lettering, as well as the odd pile of sharp sand and a pallet of bags of cement under a flapping plastic sheet. All seemingly legit builder's stuff.

The radio crackled as I made to get out.

'Oscar Seven, you POB yet?'

' 'Nother ten minutes at least, Dispatch. The traffic is fucking awful. That's F for –'

'Thank you, Oscar Seven, sod off and out.'

I hoped that would keep Dispatch off my back for a while. I had little hope that Bassotti wanted me to do a driving job for him, or at least not a kosher one and not in a minicab. I would have to think of a way to persuade Dispatch that I wasn't pocketing Bert's cash and understanding the job. That's why they hated cash customers. With account jobs they never had to check on us and the only tips we were supposed to get were a share in any waiting time the client signed for.

My client was standing behind a desk which looked as if it had been bought second-hand from some defunct government office; say the Ministry of Food *circa* 1948. There was a telephone and answerphone on the desktop and three plastic filing trays overflowing with invoices. Bassotti had his right foot up on the desk and was wiping mud off a black leather brogue with a tissue. At least the shoes were Italian.

'That Sammy shouldn't be driving a supermarket trolley.' He blinked down at his shoe, spat on the tissue and wiped some more. The Jaeger overcoat hung on a wall peg behind him, dripping mud.

'You wanted a cab?' I prompted him.

'Not exactly.' He switched feet and reached into his pocket for another tissue. 'Kelly!'

The hardboard door to the other half of the site office opened so quickly, Kelly must have been standing behind it.

She was about eighteen and living proof that you could walk, chew gum and live in Essex. She wore a purple cross-over top and mauve hot pants, with red tights underneath. She padded across the floor in a pair of Doc Martens' a policeman would have been proud of. She gave me the twice over and maybe she liked what she saw. She didn't actually spit at me.

'Look what that little turd Sammy's done.'

'Get rid of 'im, Mr B. You know 'is sort's no good. Don't know why we have to put up with 'im.'

Bassotti looked at her and blinked rapidly. 'Well, nobody's asking you, so give your brain a rest. Go get some coffee.'

Kelly chewed some more. She was probably rehearsing a sentence.

'How does yer visitor like it?' she asked, moving the weight on her hips just in case I hadn't got the message.

'Not him, you.' He went back to cleaning his shoe. 'Pretend it's your birthday. Go have a cappuccino and a sticky bun. Treat yourself out of petty cash, like you usually do.'

'I've had my break,' she moaned.

'Take another.'

'Well, if I don't finish those quotations by six o'clock, I'm not stopping late.' Her voice whined up a couple of sharps.

So she finished work at six. Subtle as a brick. Still, I filed the information away on the gift-horse principle and, to be fair, Kelly was no horse.

'Kelly,' Bert said patiently, 'don't make it two million *and one* unemployed, huh?'

'If you say so, Mr B.'

She flounced back into her office and put on a white trenchcoat, leaving the door open so I could get a last glimpse. Then a door slammed and Bassotti took his shoe off his desk.

'She'll be gone for an hour at least. Five minutes to get to the café on the corner, five to have a coffee and ten to get poked in the pantry by Luigi or Paulo or whoever's on duty.'

'Allowing five minutes to get back, what does she do with the other half-hour?'

'Puts her make-up back on. Bloody women. Bloody staff. Can't get 'em these days and when you do, can't trust 'em.'

I held out my arms.

'Ring us – we turn up. What's the job?'

Bert sat down on the one chair in the office, pushed his spectacles back on his face and blinked rapidly at me. I tried to work it out but it seemed to bear no relation to the speed at which he spoke.

'Well, I don't need a minicab for a start.'

'You ordered one and I'm here.'

'OK, an' I'll pay. Think of a job.'

'Parcel delivery to EC1?'

'That'll do. How much?'

'Thirty quid.'

'Bloody hell. All right.' He took three ten-pound notes from his wallet. 'I bet ten of that doesn't get to the company.'

'No, you're wrong there,' I said confidently. Fifteen wouldn't. 'Now what?' I asked as I palmed the cash.

'Your friend Tigger,' he said, blinking too fast to count.

'No particular friend of mine,' I said.

'Don't say you don't know 'im.'

'Oh I know him. You know I know him. Just not in the Biblical sense.'

That fazed him. He didn't blink for nearly a second.

'Well, he's done a runner.'

He waited for a reaction. I blinked at him for a change.

'So?'

'So he's done a runner with the Transit you were driving on Friday night.'

I shook my head in disbelief.

''Ang on a minute, Tigger can't drive.'

'So he said,' Bert blinked. 'But I never believed him. Did you? Everybody can drive.'

'No they can't,' I said. 'Lots of people don't drive, especially in London. If they haven't learned before they come here, the insurance alone puts them off.'

Bassotti blinked down at his shoes.

'Whatever; the little pillock never brought the keys back like he should have. I'd hate to have to report it stolen. I mean, who knows whose dabs are on it?'

'Dabs? C'mon, Bert, nobody's talked like that since the Job stopped wearing hats indoors.'

He did a double-take or, given his electric eyelids, a single-take.

'The Job – the police,' I said calmly, 'the people you are *not* going to go to in case they ask what was in the back of the van. And anyway, you'll not find a print of mine on there – finger, palm, foot or genetic.'

Bassotti pushed his spectacles back into his face again.

'So you'll help me find him then.'

'Did I say that? That's funny, I didn't feel my lips move.'

'How much?'

'There goes that echo again. I don't remember saying any-thing about helping you. If I remember right, I distinctly said it was the duty of every honest citizen to report a crime.'

'I'll give you a hundred if you find him in the next coupla days.'

'Bert – call the cops. Report the van was nicked sometime Friday. They'll assume whoever did it will have done the required cosmetic surgery by now and they won't break sweat. Get a log number off them to prove you've reported it and get on the phone to the insurance company. That's what normal people do.'

'Can't do that,' he said sullenly.

'Why not?'

'Not bleedin' insured, was it? I'll make it two-fifty if you can turn him up by Friday.'

'For two-fifty you could get somebody to lift you another van. There's a recession on, you know.'

He placed his hands palms down on the desktop.

'Look, I'm asking nicely. You've earned a few quid in the last few weeks and so has that little shitbag. Now if he's decided to play silly buggers, by my way of thinking you should help me find him – you and him being mates as it were.'

'Mates? What's all this mates shit?'

'Blood brothers you are, to hear him talk.'

'You're winding me up.'

'No, straight up. Angel this, Angel that. Two sides of the same coin, he said. He also said you were an ace driver and knew your way around. Somebody less suspicious than me might even think you put him up to it.'

'Now wait a minute. If I had, would I be daft enough to come here?'

'Maybe, maybe not. Some people have balls of brass.'

'I've had enough of this.'

I turned away from him as if disgusted and appalled at his suggestion. In fact I was checking the yard and the distance to Armstrong. There were no hod-carrying heavies blocking my escape route, that was one thing. And I wasn't scared of Bassotti himself. But then, Kelly might reappear at any time and I didn't fancy a fair fight with her. I'd already assessed that my best chance with her was coming in out of the sun swinging a sockful of sand.

'I'll make it a grand,' said Bert and there was a nervousness in his voice.

He needed me more than I needed him.

Thing was, did I need a grand?

'Hundred up front for diesel money,' I said immediately.

He reached for his wallet again.

'By Friday, remember,' he said, counting out five twenties.

'Why Friday?'

'Never you mind. Just find Tigger for me.'

'All right, all right. I'll ask around and see if I can get your van back.' I swooped on the cash. 'But this is non-returnable – OK?'

'Just find Tigger. I'll get the van back.'

'I'll try, but it won't be easy. Tigger doesn't stay long in one place.'

'Tell me something I don't know, heh?'

He rummaged in one of the in-trays until he found a sheet of notepaper. He ripped the top two inches off it and handed it to me. It was a letterhead for H.B. Builders with the address and phone number and a much-photocopied logo of a lighthouse within two circles and the legend 'Registered House Builder'.

'Ring me any time. Leave a message if I'm not here. Night or day. Any time. Just tell him I want a chat. Don't say anything about the van.'

'Finding him will be the problem,' I said.

7

So where do you start to look for someone who doesn't live anywhere or work anywhere and who probably doesn't want to be found? I didn't know; but I thought I knew a man who did.

I blagged Dispatch into thinking I was wasting my own diesel delivering parcels in the City for H.B. Builders for only fifteen pounds cash. The other fifteen pounds wasn't much, but it was tax free and in the pocket. Pocket in question: mine.

By noon I was back in Baker Street ('Sorry, Dispatch, there's something wrong with my radio. Better try another frequency. That's F for . . .') looking for Crimson. Even if he didn't know Tigger's whereabouts, he had introduced me to him and so in my book, he was down for a share of the problem. I've always hated the oil-slick public relations credo that 'if you ain't part of the solution, you're part of the problem'. According to my rules of life, if you ain't in my solution, it's your problem.

Unfortunately, Plan A failed at the off because Crimson was nowhere around. He wasn't in the McDonald's, he wasn't in the Burger King across the street. He wasn't round the corner sitting on a bike in Porter Street. And there was nobody from his dispatch outfit I could ask. Maybe they were all out on jobs and maybe I was working for the wrong firm.

I realized I was doing something wrong because although Crimson wasn't on Porter Street, the Beast from the East was. Twice in one day. I was going to have to start helping old ladies across the street, though the trouble with that these days is they think you're trying to mug them and they get the mace spray out.

'Wotcher, Angel. Skiving again?' he greeted me, parking his bike.

'Looking for somebody,' I said, sliding past him towards Armstrong.

'I heard you on the radio,' he said smugly, taking his helmet off. I hadn't noticed his single swastika earring before.

'Oh yeah? Can't stop. Might have a job on.'

'Dispatch reckons you have.'

I turned to face him. He placed his helmet in his crutch on the petrol tank and began to peel off his gauntlets.

'They think you're moonlighting – running jobs and not telling them. Asked me to let them know if I saw yer. 'Course I won't. No skin off my nose, what you're up to, though I could always use a few ready notes if there's something going down . . .'

Blackmail, from the Beast. I had no idea he had it in him. He went up a notch in my estimation, but it would take a whole turn of the ratchet to get him as high as subhuman.

'Look, Be . . . er . . . Big Fella,' I corrected once I realized I couldn't remember his name, 'there *may* be something going down and there *may* be a few readies in it. Can't say more than that. First thing I've got to do is find Crimson, you know, the kid who rides for the opposition and uses a –'

'You mean the black bastard?'

'Well . . .'

'The black bastard with the poofy friend, the one who can't stand still for two seconds?'

'Yeah, that's right, the –'

'Ain't seen him for weeks. Not that I'd give 'im the time of day.'

'Oh, well, in that case . . .'

''Course you could ask 'is bum chum. *He's* always hanging around the toilets at Baker Street with the other trouser bandits, looking for an easy mark among the dirty raincoat brigade.'

'You mean the one who can't stand still?'

'Yeah, 'im. Me and my mates 'ave our eye on him. One of these days we'll pay a call round there and sort out him and his homo friends. It's probably down to them, all these rapes on the tube, you know.'

There had indeed been a number of male rapes on the Underground that year. Not that it was unheard of, just it had been reported in the newspapers. For the Beast and his friends it had added to the homophobic hysteria which had been regenerated by some notable AIDS-related deaths in the showbiz world. Not, I imagined, that the Beast and his mates ever needed much of an excuse, but the incidents on the Underground had grown into folk legend status. Everyone had a Northern Line horror story, just like at one time, everybody *knew* the actual family which strapped a dead grandmother to the roof of the car as they went on holiday.

He looked at me and mistook the expression on my face for impressed respect. Perhaps he'd never seen gobsmacked disbelief before.

'He hangs around the gents near Platform Five every evening, 'bout rush hour. Got a mate known as Steel Rule. That says it all, don't it?'

'Do it? Does it?' I stammered.

'Notorious, 'e is,' said the Beast, showing he knew some long words. 'Smirnoff' was another one.

'Who is?'

'Steel Rule. He has one of those expanding metal rules that builders use. Has it on his belt and he stands in the next stall to you and measures what you've got.'

'You're dreaming this.' He glared at me, so I softened it and cursed myself for a coward. 'Surely you're winding me up.'

'No way. On my mother's heart.'

There he went, bragging again. If his mum had a heart she would have strangled him at birth.

'So you've seen this guy Steel Rule with Crimson?'

He had to think about this.

'No, not exactly. But I've seen him with Crimson's poofy mate loads a times, laughing and poncing about.'

'So you've been there, have you? I mean, you've used the toilets yourself, have you?'

'Only to do a recce. Like I said, me and my mates will pay

'em a visit one Saturday night and sort them out. Bloody perverts. Fancy a burger?'

'Not now. I'll catch you later.'

He shrugged, swung a leg off his bike and stomped around the corner towards McDonald's.

I looked at the Beast's shining Kawasaki and wondered what the penalty was for topping up the fuel tank with something unleaded but definitely not petrol.

And in public.

I stopped on Wigmore Street at a sandwich bar I knew, leaving Armstrong on double yellow lines.

It was only twelve-thirty but I had a choice of 'returns' at half-price. Most of the sandwich places in the West End operated the same system these days. They send a kid out on a reproduction 1920s butcher's bike to tour the neighbourhood offices with samples of their sandwiches and salads. They carried one of everything and took orders around eleven a.m. but their samples had to be returned to the kitchen for disposal, otherwise the health inspectors got shirty. The bar wasn't supposed to sell them, not after they'd been out in the traffic fumes and handled by the oiks in various accounts departments. But they made an exception for cab drivers and the money, even at half-price, didn't go through the cash register.

I took a scrambled egg and smoked salmon on brown and ate as I drove out to Barking to see Duncan the Drunken.

There were two reasons for risking a visit to Duncan's den. As probably the best car mechanic in the world, he had access to a variety of vehicles and if anyone was going to come up with a motor for Fenella's driving lessons, it would be Duncan. He also had somebody working for him who just might be able to help me on the Tigger front.

As a diehard Yorkshire nationalist, he insisted on calling lunch 'dinner' and having it at noon. If he hadn't gone to the pub afterwards, and therefore written off the rest of the day, he would be back at his workshop doing something unspeakable to an innocent punter's pride and joy.

I had long ago learned not to drop in at Duncan's house

at mealtimes. His wife, Doreen, was of the old school which regarded men as eligible for food parcels unless they were thirty pounds overweight. 'I prefer 'em plump,' she told me down the pub one night. 'There's more to hang on to and they can't run away so fast.'

Duncan was in his workshop sitting in a swivel chair with his feet on a desk in what he grandly termed his office. In reality, it was an area the size of two coffins cut off from the bays and workpits of the rest of the garage by a partition which would have been half glass if any of the glass had remained. He was reading an official-looking report with a light blue cover. As I knocked on the wooden partition and stuck my head into the office, I could read the title: PROCEEDINGS OF THE STANDING CONFERENCE ON CRIME PREVENTION IV: CAR THEFT AND INDUSTRIAL DETERRENTS. It was published by the Home Office.

'Do you know how long it takes to get into a Saab 9000i?' he asked without looking up.

'No, and I don't want to know. Good afternoon, Duncan.'

'Don't bother, you'd never get the steering lock off. A Rover's a better bet for that, though you'd have to get one with a full tank as the fuel cap gets a rating like Fort Knox.'

'Fascinating,' I said in my Mr Spock voice.

'Did you know that the Japanese are supposed to be falling behind in car alarm technology because car theft is almost unknown in Japan?' he went on.

'Well, nobody's perfect. Are you, by any chance open for business this afternoon? This year? Before the twenty-first century?'

'Bloody hell. Did you know, there are almost six hundred thousand car thefts a year and a third are done by professionals who can bypass most circuit alarms in less than three minutes? Do you know what that means?'

'Sure. It means that four hundred thousand cars are nicked by amateurs, giving people like you a bad name.'

'Ha-bloody-ha. Very funny. Did you want summat?'

Letting his native Yorkshire accent slip, he flung down the Home Office report and swung his feet off the desk.

I pointed at the report.

'Does it give a rating for small cars which withstand body-work impacts up to twenty miles-an-hour, that do a hundred to the gallon and have the best handbrakes?'

He thought about that for a moment, reached inside his shirt and scratched his chest and said with a grin: 'You've been conned into giving driving lessons, haven't yer? You poor daft pillock. Hope she's worth it.'

'Look,' I pleaded, 'I'm in enough trouble without getting the verbals from you. What you got?'

His grin slid sideways into an ominous smile and he came and put an arm around me.

'Angel, you are the luckiest bugger I know.'

'I'm not going to like this, am I?'

'Nonsense! You, for once, are the right man in the right place at the right time. I've got just the thing you need.'

'If you really have, you might as well know I can't afford it.'

'Don't talk daft. Local driving school just changing over cars. I've got a two-year-old Metro *with dual control*, would you believe? All I have to do is strip out the extra controls and ring the clock back and – wallop! – into the old car auction. Nice clean car, one lady owner.'

'How do you get one lady owner if it's been used by a driving school?'

'It's in Doreen's name now. The last owner was one lady – geddit? We've already done a spray job and got rid of the driving school logo but I can slap on some "L" plates for you.

'Hey – did you hear about the Irishman who was the first one in his village to get a car? He had the "L" plates on and after the first lesson somebody said "What's that mean, Paddy?" and Paddy says "Learner". And after the second lesson, he has a "G.B." sticker on the back and they ask him what that means, and he says "Getting Better". Geddit? What's up, heard it before?'

'Bound to have, but you can't always remember the good ones, can you?' I smiled as I said it. I had to; I hadn't conned him about the car yet. 'So what would you let me borrow the Metro for?'

'Fair words and money, as me old dad used to say.'

'I've got no money, Duncan, but I have two very fair words: lock gun.'

'Aah,' said Duncan slowly, 'I was wondering when you'd bring that up.'

A few months before I had come into possession of an electronic lock gun which, had it been available in Britain at all, would have been tightly restricted to the police or a handful of legitimate breakdown or vehicle recovery companies. I had shown it to Duncan and, purely out of professional interest, he had agreed to look after it for me. I had never seen it again and it hadn't been mentioned since, but he knew he owed me one. And I knew he knew I knew.

'So we're not exactly in a money-changing-hands situation here?'

'Got it in one, Duncan.'

'How long are you gonna need it for?'

'That's a good question. Say two nights a week plus a Saturday or Sunday.'

'Yeah, but for how long? I was supposed to sell the bloody thing some time this year. Who is it you're teaching anyway?'

'Fenella.'

He covered his eyes with his right hand.

'I'm getting one of me headaches.'

'I think I might have one by tonight,' I said, the full horror of what I'd agreed to finally sinking in. 'When can I pick it up?'

'Say six o'clock.'

'Sounds good. One other thing – is Maxi around?'

That brought a sparkle to his eyes. He knew me better than to have to give his hands-off speech about Maxi, who was rapidly gaining pride of place in Duncan and Doreen's household, maybe even ahead of his favourite monkey wrench or his pewter tankard down the local pub. I was well aware of how much she meant to them, just like I was aware of how easily Duncan's horseshoe hands would fit around my windpipe.

'I want to ask her advice on something,' I said casually. 'That's all.'

'She's in the pit,' said Duncan, jerking a thumb into the workshop.

I narrowed my eyes to get used to the gloom. The only electric light was a bulb in a wire cage on a length of cable which was clipped to the axle of the car parked over the inspection pit.

'She loves working on the Cosworth. Would do it for no pay, she said. Great car,' Duncan mused. 'Ever fancied one?'

'Not really,' I said truthfully. I admired the Ford Cosworth but so did every joyrider in town and they were such a target now the insurance premiums were stratospheric.

'If I ever drove one,' I conceded, 'it would be the S.E. Cosworth.'

Duncan looked puzzled.

'Someone Else's,' I explained.

He grinned. 'I'll remember that one when I sell the bugger.'

'Make sure you fit an alarm.'

'And an engine disabler. Maxi's on to it. Oi! Maxi! Visitor.'

There was a scraping of boots down in the brick-lined pit and Maxi used the front bumper of the car to heave herself out until she sat on the edge. Then she took a rag from her oil-stained overalls and wiped her fingerprints from the bumper. With me, that would have been a precaution. For her, it was a mark of respect for the car.

She nodded her close-cropped head in my direction just the once. That was her shorthand for saying hello, she was fine, she hoped I was and could she get back to work now? Her hands fell silent in her lap.

Duncan had stumbled across her, literally, in a jeweller's doorway one night in the City. Quite what Duncan was planning to do in the shop doorway was never resolved. What Maxi was doing was a fair crack at suicide by solvent abuse and hypothermia.

Duncan took her home and Doreen put her in a bath to soak off a filthy red T-shirt which had stuck to her chest there was so much glue down the front of it. Then she had fed her up and talked non-stop at her for a month, not getting a word in reply.

One day Maxi followed Duncan to his garage and just hung out there, watching him work. The way he tells it, he was reaching from under the hood of a car for a socket spanner and the correct-sized socket was handed to him. He invited her to help him finish the tune-up or whatever and that afternoon she had her own pair of overalls and a name – Maxi – because that was the car she'd been working on. If she ever told him her real name, or anything else about herself, Duncan had never let on.

I crouched down, almost sitting on my heels, so I would be nearer eye level and less threatening.

'Hiya, Maxi. Listen, no pressure, OK? I need some advice.'

There was no response but she was still sitting there and that I took as a plus.

'I'm trying to find someone – a young guy – lives on the street . . .'

An eye flicked. She had expected me to say 'like you did'.

'He moves around a lot. Lincoln's Inn, the Strand. Knows a lot of people. Calls himself Tigger.'

'Gay scene?' she said quietly.

'Could be. Don't know if he's a regular.'

'Rent boy?' She said this staring straight ahead at the Cosworth.

'Could be. You heard the name?'

'No.' Was that too quick? I couldn't tell. She'd said more to me so far than she ever had before.

'Why did you say rent boy then?' I asked gently.

'It's always the renters they come looking for. Frightened they're gonna tell on somebody, or demand money from them. Sometimes they want to find them again because they like them, or want to give them a present or something. But usually it's to keep them quiet.'

'It's nothing like that – look, I'm a mate of Tigger's and I just need to find him. It's about a van, that's all. No sweat. We did some jobs together. I just don't know how to find him.'

She looked at me and began to edge her buttocks back

into the pit. I was losing her in more ways than one.

'Does he have money, this Tigger?'

'Some.'

'And he's on the street from choice?'

'I guess so.'

'Then he doesn't want to be found.'

She was gone.

There was enough of the afternoon left to get back to the West End and do a couple of parcel jobs for Dispatch just to keep in with the firm. None of them would put me in profit as far as they were concerned but times were hard and there were a lot of owner-drivers queuing up for vacancies.

My mind wasn't on the job, though to be fair it never had been. What exercised me was partly what Maxi had said, but mostly where the hell I could take Fenella for her first (uninsured) driving lesson. That was a tricky one – I mean, there are so few nuclear testing grounds devoid of anything other than single-cell life forms in London these days.

I was cruising Marylebone Road when I had my first bit of luck of the day. A rider on a flash BMW cut me up and gave me a swivel of his backside as he settled in front of Armstrong. The rider was invisible in leathers and helmet but I recognized the bike and wondered for the millionth time how Crimson could afford a machine like that. I flashed Armstrong's headlights (no horn: that means war in taxi land) and he flipped an indicator before turning right into Baker Street.

I followed him until he pulled into Porter Street and I was parked and out of Armstrong by the time he'd got his helmet off.

'Yo, Angel-man, how they hanging?' he greeted me.

'A lot more comfortably if you can tell me where to find Tigger.'

Crimson's eyes shot up to heaven.

'O-oh. What's he done now?'

'Nothing serious, just run out on a job and I gotta find him.'

'That guy is the wind, man,' said Crimson, peeling off his gauntlets.

'I thought you knew him.'

'He's been around. You know. Here, there. Don't mess with him myself, 'cos I've got my reputation to think of. Ain't seen him for weeks.'

I flapped my arms and reconsidered the benefits of smoking heavily.

'When you don't want him around, you can't get rid of him but when you try to find him, nobody's got a clue.'

'Sounds like Tigger,' Crimson nodded sagely. 'You tried any of his regular hang-outs?'

'No, I seem to have mislaid my copy of the *Good Cardboard Box Guide*.'

'Aw shit, you'll never find him on the street. I meant the places he hangs out, not where he lays his head.'

'Such as?'

'There's the pub up East on Rimmer Road.'

'The Grapes?'

'Yeah, that's the one. He's been there more than once.'

So had I and now the sign above the bar came back to me: GAY NIGHT LASER KARAOKE.

'I know the place. I've even been there with him.'

'Ask around, man, but expect some strange and wicked answers.'

'I thought you were going to give me one.'

'What?'

'A strange answer. When you said regular hang-outs I thought you were gonna recommend the gents on Platform Five round the corner.'

'You've been talking to the Beast, ain't you?'

I nodded.

'He's got a thing about that place. I think he musta had a close encounter there himself. You got time for a tea or summfing?'

He pointed to the McDonald's sign.

'Naw, I've got a driving lesson to give.'

'Suit yourself, man. Good luck finding Tigger. Live long

and prosper and all that shit. Oh — and don't believe one word the Beast tells you.'

'I won't,' I said, taking out Armstrong's keys. 'Not even the bit about the Steel Rule guy who trawls the toilets.'

Crimson grinned.

'Yeah, I heard him tell that one before but it's all shit. They ain't got steel rules in their pockets. Man, they're just genuinely pleased to see you.'

'Angel, we're home. Angel, say something. Did I do all right? Angel, say something. Anything. Please . . .'

8

There was a sign in one of the windows of the Grapes saying: BAR STAFF WANTED. It was hand-written on a piece of cardboard torn from a box, but at least the spelling was fair. I hadn't noticed it on my previous visit. Maybe it hadn't been there before, or maybe the Grapes was the sort of pub where it was better not to notice things.

I had arrived earlier than intended, around seven p.m. I had been determined not to hang around the house in Stuart Street in case Fenella spotted me and demanded another lesson, so I had nipped in, fed Springsteen, told him to take messages, and sneaked out again. Now I was sitting in Armstrong in the car park waiting for some inspiration.

The only train of thought I had was that Tigger had asked for a meet here at eight p.m. that first night I met Bassotti. I knew he slept up West, or at least that's where he'd always asked me to drop him, so perhaps if he used the pub he used it early. Until I saw the sign asking for staff, that had been my one and only cunning plan, ploy and tactic.

The blag of going in to ask about a job at least gave me the option of hanging around inside and chatting up the manager. That solved one problem, as gay night audiences don't welcome outsiders as a rule, especially not snooping ones asking questions. And who can blame them. They were there to party, not provide a free floor show or missing person service.

One bar had been reserved for the festivities by placing in front of the door a life-size cut-out of Humphrey Bogart as he appeared in *Casablanca*. Across his white dinner jacket, in what appeared to be lipstick (Sunset Gash was the shade, I think) was written 'Gay Nite Tonite'. Then, lower down:

'This could be the start of a beautiful friendship.' Was nothing sacred?

Beyond Bogie I could see a guy in a tank top assembling the disco gear, complete with autocue for the karaoke. Beyond him, with her back to me, was a tall blonde emptying plastic bags of coins into the cash register as a float. I decided to take my chances with her.

'Excuse me,' I said to the back of her *Basic Instinct* haircut.

She looked up into the mirror behind the bar.

'I think you want the other bar,' she said in an Australian accent.

'Actually, I'm looking for the manager.'

'Really?' She went on emptying coins into the register. 'Well, actually, sport, you've found her. 'Bout the job is it?'

'Yeah. What's the form? I could use a few nights, no weekends and cash in hand.'

'Sounds good to me. Let me know if you find anyone hiring.'

There was an ugly buzz as the cash register told everyone that its drawer had been open too long and there was probably some fiddle going on. She closed it with her right hip as she turned.

'Look, everything here's on the up, OK? We're looking for full-timers and we'll go to a hundred and forty pounds a week after tax, plus your grub, plus accommodation, we are that desperate. Average length of stay is three months. You do split shifts four days, one night Friday thru Sunday, two days off per fortnight on a rota basis. Interested?'

'I was looking for part-time,' I said weakly, wondering how to string the conversation out to maybe half a minute.

'Sorry, nothing doing. Did the Jobcentre send you?'

Jobcentre? I almost asked what she was talking about.

'No, I just saw the sign.'

She gave me a good once-over with eyes which could have microwaved pizza.

'Done bar work before?'

'Sure. And cellar work. Don't expect any Tom Cruise fancy cocktails but I can manage a lager top and a Malibu with ice without losing track of what day it is.'

'Got references?'

'Can get 'em, or give you some numbers to bell. A couple of pubs down Southwark and the odd wine bar in the City.' Very odd, now I remembered.

'Got any ID?'

Now that threw me and I gave her a lights-on-but-nobody-home look, then remembered I had a driving licence in my wallet and handed it over. As she read the name on it, I twigged. She thought I was from the Jobcentre or Social Security or somewhere, checking up.

'Roy MacLean,' she said.

Yes, those were some of my names.

'Are you gay?'

I flashed back with a lightning, witty response: 'No, of course not.'

'OK, tell you what I'll do. I'll take you on as a relief because I'm short-handed tonight. If that goes all right, then we'll see, but if anybody asks, you're a relief barperson from the agency.'

'Which agency? Just in case . . .'

'If anyone asks that, come see me quick. I'm April, but I'll be in the other bar most of the evening. You'll work this one with Sam and Dave. I'll take you upstairs and get you a white shirt and bow tie – sorry, house rule. Sam'll tell you the others. I'll pay you three pounds an hour, starting at eight o'clock. Nobody leaves till the glasses are dry and cash register balances. Keep your mouth shut unless absolutely necessary and do what Sam and Dave tell you. You can have two five-minute cigarette breaks away from the bar, preferably outside. If anyone offers you a drink, say you'll have half a lager and take the right money. Don't try and screw tips and don't let me catch you drinking it.'

'Anything else?'

'Yeah. Don't let me find you've got any bad attitudes. I don't employ gays on gay nights. It keeps life simpler. But no interaction with the customers, OK? No lip, no toilet jokes, no references to AIDS. You know anything about AIDS?'

'You can't catch it from beer glasses. The washing-up water is hot enough to kill the virus.'

She was impressed, I could tell.

'That's good. Anything you need to know?'

'I think you've covered everything.'

Sam and Dave turned out to be sisters.

Samantha and Davina, wouldn't you know it, and they were only filling in as barpersons because their real vocation was as a singing duo, sometimes a cappella, sometimes with their cousin Henry and his synthesizer, sometimes fronting third-rate pub jazz bands as a budget version of the Andrews Sisters. Most times unemployed and back to bar work. Professionally, they called themselves Sam and Dave but they'd met several agents and recording managers who said they couldn't use that name. It was something to do with someone else who had got in first way back in history. I agreed it was before my time too, whatever they were talking about. I knew that, genetically, they at least had to have a brain cell between them.

In the staff room above the bar, Dave showed me the clean laundry bag which had a selection of freshly washed but rarely ironed white shirts. I asked for a 15-inch collar and she gave me a 16½-inch one, explaining that it got hot and sweaty later on. I said I hoped so as I let her help me button it up and she smiled encouragingly.

Sam chose a clip-on bow tie for me and offered to fit it as there wasn't a mirror. She told me it was safer than the real tie-on ones or even the ones on elastic (the pub had a comprehensive choice) in case anyone grabbed it.

'So things can get a bit lively, can they?' I asked.

'Sometimes,' said Sam.

'Most times,' said Dave.

I watched as they adjusted each other's bow ties.

'But I can rely on you two to protect me, can't I?' I gave them the full teeth smile. No cheap dental work there.

Dave shook her short blonde hair at me.

'We were hoping you'd watch our backs, actually.'

I thought about this.

'Do the customers get a bit aggressive?'

'Some of them you'd think had never seen red meat,' said Sam.

Then they both giggled.

I must have looked as bemused as I felt. Dave patted me on the cheek.

'Don't worry, we have confidence in you, Roy. It is Roy, isn't it?'

'Yes, but what do you mean confidence? Why should . . . ?'

A look of genuine surprise crossed her face.

'April didn't tell you, did she? Tuesday is *female* gay night.'

'No, she must have forgotten to mention that.'

The bar began to fill to the raucous tones of L7, the all-female Californian band, in heavy mood. At least nobody was going to get up and karaoke along with them. There was no sign of the disc jockey who had been setting up. He'd set up, put on a tape and done a runner.

'You'll have to do the rounds for dirty glasses and ashtrays,' Sam advised me.

'You'll be safe,' Dave chipped in. 'You've got something in your trousers.'

'Watch it, Sis,' warned Sam. Then to me: 'April doesn't allow us to cheek off the customers, so no lip – however much they wind you up.'

I did a quick scan of the spirits on the back bar, their prices marked on small white stickers the size of postage stamps. Beneath them were four glass-door fridges stuffed with imported lagers and bottles of white wine with the corks drawn.

'Biggest sellers are the beers by the neck, no glass,' said Sam pushing behind me. 'A few of the Vanilla Dykes go for white wine spritzers and the older GBs may hit the spirits later on.'

'GBs?' I queried as she thrust a lemon, a paring knife and a saucer at me.

'Gender Benders. Start slicing.'

I made a note to add that one to Duncan's Irish driver joke.

'And what about —?'

'Customer,' hissed Dave. 'Your end.'

At the far end of the bar was a woman nervously puffing on a cigarette. She wore a huge, chunky-knit cardigan, which could possibly have housed a small family, but apart from that, looked perfectly normal.

I approached and did the universal barman's quizzical stare.

I thought it best not to speak.

'Southern Comfort and Malibu, please,' she said politely.

'Ice? Lemon?' I risked.

'Both, thank you.' She puffed out a small smokescreen.

I moved to the optics and made the drinks expertly, or so I thought, placing them in front of her with a flourish.

'That'll be —'

I had even worked out the right price, but I never got a chance to tell her.

'No! No!'

Even in the disco lights, she'd gone pale. Then she drew on her cigarette violently, blew smoke at me and shook her head.

Then she said, 'No, no, no,' turned on her heels and walked away.

I sensed Sam at my side.

'What? What did I do wrong?'

She reached over and picked up the drinks.

'In the same glass, you idiot.'

She poured the Malibu into the Southern Comfort and took the empty glass away. Somebody shouted for a pint of lager and I turned to get that, remembering not to ask if they wanted a strawberry in it or anything. When I looked back, the full glass at the end of the bar had gone and the correct money stood in a small pile of coins.

It was going to be one hell of a learning curve.

Two and a half lager tops. Molson Dry, please. Three tonic waters, no ice, she's cold enough. Beck's. Two Sols, don't forget the lime, though he doesn't look like he knows where to put it. Two pints of lager, a dry sherry and a whisky and Lucozade. Bailey's with ice. What do you mean you haven't any Lucozade? Pils with the top off. So how much was the whisky without the Lucozade? Half a shandy. A grapeka — it's vodka and grapefruit juice, don't you know anything, you git? Quick, put a large gin in there while she's not looking. Don't you do Chardonnay? A Southern Comfort and a Malibu, please. Of course I want two glasses, you prawn!

It was going rather well. But it couldn't last.

Dave sounded the alarm in a hiss of genuine panic.

'Phasers on stun! Watch yourself, Roy, it's Thelma and Louise.'

I had no idea what she was talking about but I had more sense than to stop and look. Avoiding eye contact had got me through the first hour and a half but now the disco had given way to the karaoke and a procession of volunteers were queuing up to take the microphone and sing along to k.d. lang. Those not interested or, let's face it, embarrassed by the amateur offerings, began to scramble for the seats as far away from the karaoke gear as possible. Two of them had found bar stools from somewhere and were staking a claim to the end of the bar where I'd had my first customer.

I risked a glance at them while bending down to clean off an ashtray with a paint brush. One was a redhead, the other a blonde with blue streaks, the same blue as you get on a shirt when a fountain pen leaks. Both had it cropped to within a half-inch of the skull except for a comma-shaped lock over the left eye. The redhead wore large round glasses with red frames and the blonde had one gold stud in her left nostril.

Nothing out of the ordinary there.

'Better see what Iron Tits and Steel Arse want,' hissed Sam. 'I ain't going near them. You're on your own, kid.'

'Hey, what's . . . ?'

But there was no way I would get anything out of them except a view of the back of their heads.

'Lousy service around here,' somebody said loudly.

'Men always give lousy service, darling, didn't you know?'

Action stations. Keep it civil.

'Being served?'

I didn't say 'girls', I didn't say 'ladies'. I didn't ask the redhead if she enjoyed eating lemons whole as surely nothing else could have put that expression on her face. I wanted to keep my job.

'Two Rollicking Balls,' said the redhead.

'Pardon?'

'Deaf as well,' said the blonde.

They stared at me. Somewhere behind the lasers, the karaoke microphone changed hands and another song started. It didn't help.

'I asked for a pair of Rollicks,' said the redhead.

'I know what you said,' I muttered quietly to myself. 'I just don't know which language we're talking.'

Sam got me out of it. She coughed loudly and I shot a glance over my shoulder, to catch her waggling a foot at one of the cold cabinets as she tried to hand two pints over the bar without spilling. Her foot was pointing to the cooler containing the imported beers selection.

'Two Rolling Rocks coming right up,' I announced.

'The penny seems to have dropped,' said the redhead.

'A-fucking-mazing,' said the blonde.

I gave them their change and looked around desperately for some other customers. Where were they when you wanted them? Watching an overweight middle-aged woman in twin set and sensible shoes doing 'My Way'. Sinatra has a lot to answer for.

'You should go out and collect some glasses,' Dave said with a grin.

'Sod off.'

That would have meant asking Thelma and Louise to remove their elbows from the bar flap so I could get out. And then asking them if I could come back in. No way. Not while they had bottles in their hands. I had no intention of even looking in their direction, but it soon became clear that I had been elected as target for tonight.

'I don't know why I ever bothered with men,' said the redhead far too loudly. 'They are universal wastes of space.'

I edged my way up the bar looking for glasses to dry or

olives to stone or anything. A woman loomed out of the light show and I was about to serve her when Dave muscled in front of me, elbowing me back down the bar.

'The last man I had,' the redhead was saying, 'stripped off while I was making coffee in the kitchen. I wander in, balancing a cafetière and two mugs, and there he is but he's still got his socks on! Would you believe it?'

'So what did you do?' asked the blonde as if she hadn't heard it before.

'I put the coffee down and looked at what he had on offer and said I didn't realize it was so cold in here and offered to turn the heating up.'

The blonde laughed.

'Is that why he kept his socks on?'

'It was the only thing he was getting on that night, I can tell you.'

More hilarity.

'And then, then' – the redhead choked on her Rolling Rock – 'he looks down and it starts to shrink before his very eyes! Talk about two onions stuck on a cocktail stick! And . . . and . . . he has the nerve to say size isn't important!'

'Who told him that?' the blonde hooted.

Another man, I thought, but kept it to myself.

'You know Simone?' said the blonde.

'All sixteen stone of her?' the redhead giggled.

'Yes, and fifteen of them are round her arse!' The blonde gasped for breath. 'Well, she told me – after she'd had a few – that she once picked up a man and tried to do it in a shop doorway!'

'Go on, never!'

'It's true. The only trouble was he was as pissed as she was and neither of them could go through the motions. She said it was like trying to put an oyster in a slot machine!'

'Oi! Tinkerballs!'

That was me.

'More Rollerballs.'

I flipped the tops off two more bottles and the redhead proffered a five-pound note and a killer look, defying me to stare her out. I ducked her gaze, got her change and planted it on the bar in front of her, keeping my eyes on my trainers.

'When I think of what I used to do because of *men*,' she said to her partner. 'Like worrying about my weight, for Christ's sake. Every morning, first thing, on the bathroom scales. And an ounce or two over would bring on Toxic Shock syndrome.'

'I hope you remembered to have a pee before you weighed yourself,' said the blonde.

'Have a pee? Jesus, I used to shave my legs before getting on!'

A fingernail jabbed me in the arm. It was Dave wearing a cherubic smile which didn't fool me one bit.

'We're running out of vodka. Nip into the other bar and ask April for a bottle.'

'You do it.'

'I'm busy and you're the new boy and April doesn't like disobedience.'

I looked towards the danger zone. Thelma and Louise were draining their beers. I reached for two more as the redhead snapped her fingers at me.

'I may be gone some time,' I hissed at Dave.

'I even used to shave my armpits in those days,' the redhead started up again.

I gave her her change and began to wipe the bar counter with a damp cloth. It's an old trick perfected by bored barmen, as when you ask people to lift their glasses, most will take a drink before putting them down again. Most men will probably finish them. Consequently, you speed up the drinking rate and sell more.

'You were worried about the weight of your underarm hair?' asked the blonde, lifting her bottle. 'Now that's what I call paranoid.'

'No, no, no,' said the redhead. 'You shaved there because men expected it. Don't ask me why.'

I said, 'Excuse me' ever so politely and lifted the bar flap. They made no attempt to move their bar stools and I had a gap of about three inches to squeeze through.

'Men are funny about body hair,' said the redhead and I

was so close now I could smell the Rolling Rock on her breath.

'It used to worry me a lot . . .'

I let the bar flap descend behind me, as I eased between them.

'I mean, what does one do' – she was really loud in my ear now – 'with unwanted pubic hair?'

'Spit it out,' I said, diving towards the door.

'I know you've got your new job to go to at the pub, Angel,' said Fenella sulkily. 'But I think a proper lesson should be more than five minutes.'

Was that all it had been? I'd smoked three cigarettes.

'Setting off and parking are very important components of the driving test,' I lectured her.

'But I thought we might have made it out of our street.'

Two lessons and she was hooked, raring to have a go at roundabouts, T-junctions, three-point turns. She had even bought a copy of the Highway Code without Lisabeth noticing and was secretly identifying road signs and already getting her knickers in a twist in case they asked her the one about the countdown markers approaching an unmanned level crossing without gates.

'We'll do more at the weekend,' I promised as I locked the car and looked down the road to where Armstrong was parked.

Fenella checked the entrance to Number Nine to make sure there was no sign of Lisabeth.

'I said I was going to the library, so if she asks, say you gave me a lift, OK? Otherwise she'll wonder what I'm doing back so soon.'

'Anything you say, but you know how I hate to deceive people, Fenella.'

'Just this once, eh?' She squeezed my arm.

'Just this once,' I sighed.

'Thanks. And I'm sorry I didn't know what a Vanilla Dyke was.'

'Forget it,' I said generously. It had been a long shot.

'But I'll ask Lisabeth later on.'

'Er . . . no,' I stammered. 'Don't do that.'

Fenella hit the street and was in at the front door like a rat up a drainpipe. I was locking Armstrong when I heard the communal phone ringing from inside. Sure enough, it was for me.

Fenella was holding the receiver at arm's length and mouthing what appeared to be 'Mister Bastard'. I didn't quite believe my eyes, reading that on her lips, but then again, it could cover any one of a number of my friends. I took the phone from her and she said, 'Thanks for the lift, Angel!' very loudly so that Lisabeth could hear upstairs, and she said it again as she went up herself.

'Yo, Angel,' I said, expecting it to be Bunny, or Duncan the Drunken, or some other reprobate.

'Bert Bassotti here,' came an echoing voice. He was on an amplified office phone, the sort where you could use your hands for several other purposes.

'Hello there, Bert, you sound kinda distant. What can I do for you?'

I was more worried about how he had got my number, but then that was probably via Tigger. I wasn't too worried. It is still tricky enough to get someone's address from just a phone number unless you're a cop or similar. Not impossible, but tricky.

'Wondered if you'd made any progress,' said Bassotti, still sounding as if he was sky-diving into the Grand Canyon. There was only one explanation; someone was listening in.

'Got a couple of leads, Bert. Something I think I can follow up tomorrow night looks especially good.'

But if you think I'm telling you about gay laser karaoke nights, you've another think coming.

'I just want to make it clear that we stressed that there was some urgency about this job, Roy. Didn't we?'

'Of course, Mr Bassotti,' I said, servile, noting the 'Roy' — and also the 'we' all of a sudden.

'So you think you can come up with something? By Friday, that is?'

'Friday was the day I was aiming for,' I lied. 'I'm doing my best. I take it the finder's fee still stands?'

Down the line came a distant laugh, but even at that distance I could tell it was unpleasant.

'Yeah, finder's fee. That still stands.'

'Then I'll do my best, Mr Bassotti.'

'You do that, Roy. You do that.'

I never did get to experience the male gay laser karaoke night that Thursday, as I had a piece of luck.

I turned up for work and got a blast from April about trying not to upset the punters – sorry, customers – this time, before being allowed upstairs to find a clean white shirt and a bow tie.

Sam and Dave were not on duty until later and I was told to get the bar ready for opening with a tall, gangling youth called Keith and a wild-eyed Irishman called Joe who said nothing, just sat on an upturned beer crate pulling alternately on a joint and a can of Special Brew.

Keith nervously tried to make friends, relieved that he would not be working alone with Joe.

'I don't normally do bar work,' he said hesitantly. 'I'm really here to help Derek with the disco and the karaoke gear.'

Joe grunted something unintelligible.

'Oh yeah?' I said, feigning interest.

'My friend Derek's really good at it. Disco, I mean.'

'Uh-huh.'

'He's been a regular here for three years. Knows everybody.'

'Does he now? Come and introduce me.'

Derek was sorting out CDs for the disco and, rarity these days, he also had some vinyl LPs. I checked a few covers: mostly Dusty Springfield and the Beverley Sisters.

I told Keith to bottle up and fetch in some more cases of beer. He was younger than me, needed the exercise and seemed happy to help.

'Keith says you know most of this crowd,' I tried on Derek.

'Could say that, I s'pose.'

He was trying to be cool but made the fatal error of wearing a T-shirt carrying the name and sign of the pub. (Rule of Life

No. 51: Never wear a T-shirt in the place it commemorates.)
The T-shirt I'd been wearing when I arrived advertised a
home-brew pub in Soquel, California, further removed from
the Grapes in Rimmer Road you could not imagine.

'Ever come across my old mate Tigger?'

'Cheeky little toerag, doesn't know when to quit?'

'That's him.'

'Ain't seen him for weeks.'

He busied himself loading the CD player.

'But I copped his partner this morning.'

I wasn't sure if this was a test or not. If I knew Tigger, I'd
surely know his partner, wouldn't I? Or maybe Derek was
just bad with names.

'Lee? How is he these days?'

I couldn't tell whether that had reassured him or not.

'Yeah, Lee the Smackhead, as he's known. Seemed straight
this morning and had a bit of dosh on him. Bought himself
a tent and was moving in.'

'Where?'

'The Fields. Lincoln's Inn. God knows why, there's an
injunction or something that means they're all going to have
to get out soon.'

'Yeah, so I'd heard.'

Derek began rearranging his light show and I left him to
it.

I left Keith bottling up and I left April still needing bar
staff.

I ran upstairs and grabbed my jacket and T-shirt. Joe was
still sitting there, popping another can. I smiled at him and
he glared at me.

As I went through the bar, I told Keith I was just nipping
out to my car. I got into Armstrong and drove away.

I never did get paid for the Tuesday shift. But then, they
never got their shirt and bow tie back.

9

Bassotti had said there was a grand in it for me if I found Tigger by Friday. Derek's lead about Lincoln's Inn was the only thing I'd come up with all week and tomorrow was Friday. So I checked that the flashlight I kept in Armstrong's boot was working and I headed west.

It was dark and raining by the time I made Holborn. It was the quiet time there, around nine p.m., with few people on the street and dozens of taxis with their signs on cruising up and down. You could tell there was a recession on: empty taxis and queues at the bus stops even though it was raining. Funny, though, that in two hours when the pubs emptied out, you wouldn't find a cab for love nor money.

I cut round the back of the Fields and parked illegally on Portugal Street. I rummaged around in the boot some more until I found a California Angels baseball cap to combat the rain, and while looking I came across a pair of plastic diesel pump gloves. Those went on too. You never knew.

I entered the Fields themselves from the south-east end. They aren't fields as such, of course. Fields are big green things which wave in the wind and live beyond the M25 motorway and are eligible for European Community subsidies. Lincoln's Inn Fields is really a big lawn with a crisscross path and iron railings round the perimeter. It is flanked by Lincoln's Inn itself, where the legal beagles hang out, and the Royal College of Surgeons, where the medics pontificate on the health of the nation. It is home to a movable population of the homeless, many of whom are sick and all probably breaking the law.

I was holding my torch down at the side of my leg, my thumb on the flash on/off button. It reminded me of drinking sessions years ago in Southwark with an old robber called High Interest, who used to hold a pickaxe handle that way while waiting in the queue for a cashier to come free. He maintained he'd once waited twenty minutes like that, edging his way forward, and nobody had said a word until he started smashing at the cashier's glass window. That was in the days before video cameras, of course, and he couldn't ever have been a very successful robber; after all, he used to drink with me and live in Southwark. He was called High Interest because he specialized in Building Societies, but that was the most imaginative thing about him.

The largest concentration of tents and makeshift bashas were in the corner to my left, though in total there were no more than a dozen of them. At one time there were supposed to be nearly two hundred people living here but harassment, fear and the winter had thinned them out much more successfully than the government's attempts at rehousing.

In the centre of the Fields was the bandstand, or the folly, or the gazebo. It had many names, including Timothy Whites after an ageing newspaper columnist had suggested that more drugs changed hands there than in a branch of the former high street chemists. That was not on my agenda if I could avoid it. Derek had said he'd seen Lee with a tent; though even if the tent was there, it didn't mean Lee was.

I played the beam of the torch on to the ground between the path and the nearest tents. Most had well-worn muddy tracks thanks to the rain. The furthest two did not, therefore they were the recent arrivals. Much more of this, I thought, and I might consider reapplying to the Scouts, assuming they'd forgotten a particular incident twenty years ago.

A black cab went round the square. He was empty but not showing a light on his meter. In the beam of his headlights I could make out the detail of the tents, one a standard four-corner guy rope affair, the other a light blue dome tent shaped like an igloo. It was impossible to tell if either was inhabited. That was the weird thing about the Fields, it was so quiet.

The only sound I'd heard had been a creaking and then a soft thud from the folly in the centre of the Fields. The dwellers there had long since learned not to draw attention to themselves after dark. Hence, there were few lights. Nobody gave dinner parties round here.

My eyes were as accustomed to the dark as they ever would be and I wasn't finding anything out standing there on the path but I was increasing the chances of being spotted as an intruder.

From somewhere behind me, I heard glass break, followed by a wail of obscenities. That spurred me on. Keeping the beam of the torch aimed just in front of my feet, I crept towards the nearest tent, the grass squelching underfoot.

A yard away from its zippered fly sheet I thought I could hear voices from inside. Two voices, banter going back and forth, but the words indistinct under the patter of the rain on the canvas. I went down in a crouch and strained to try and make out the murmurs. In truth I had no idea what to do next. I was badly in need of a doorbell or a piece of wood to knock on.

I shook some rain out of my ears and tilted my head nearer the tent flap. I began to make out some words. It was almost as if whoever was in there was playing a game like 'I Spy' or something. One of them tossing out an idea, the other answering.

'. . . drinking out of a chipped cup . . .'

'. . . medium to low . . .'

'. . . bath together . . .'

'. . . low risk . . .'

'. . . anal intercourse . . .'

'. . . outstanding risk . . . How am I doing?'

'. . . a minute . . . few more yet. Strawberry flavoured condoms.'

'Low risk. What . . . hey! Visitors!'

'Who's there?'

There was a scuffling from inside the tent, then a clanging of metal on metal which sounded like nothing I'd heard before.

'Er . . . sorry to intrude,' I said, knowing it sounded lame, 'but I'm looking for a guy called Lee.'

There was a silence while they considered this.

'Piss off,' came a voice pretending to be deeper than natural.

I hadn't expected a warm welcome but it wasn't as if I was trying to sell them a conservatory or double glazing.

'Sorry to disturb you. Incidentally, they're high risk.'

More scuffling and more silence.

'Strawberry flavoured condoms. They're higher risk than you'd think. Most of them don't come up to British Standard specification. It says in very small print that they are for amusement only and not to be used as an effective barrier. Most people just hear "condom" and assume it must be low risk.'

Another cab zipped round the square, his headlights filtered through the railings. If he saw me, he didn't slow down. Why should he? There I was, kneeling in the rain at night having a perfectly sensible conversation with an apparently empty tent, in an historic square in the heart of the most civilized capital city in the world. All I was trying to do was score points in the 'High Risk/Low Risk' game everybody was playing with one of the latest generation of helpful pamphlets from the health authorities. Get in on their wavelength. Indicate that I was informed and concerned.

'Piss off.'

I never need telling three times. I squelched over to the dome tent and as this was the last dwelling on that side of the Fields, I risked more of the torch. There was no light from the tent, but I could make out the door flap wasn't closed properly.

There was also definitely someone at home. I could tell by the smell.

I crouched down near to the door, but to the side and held the torch ready to either flick on or brain somebody with.

'Lee?' I said quietly, then louder when I got no response.

'Lee, I'm a mate of Tigger's, OK?' I tried. Still nothing.

I bit the bullet and loosened the tent flap and shone the torch inside.

At first I thought he was a stiff, an overdose at least, at worst the victim of a maniac serial killer who collected not just heads but the top half of the whole torso. All I could take in to begin with were the hi-top trainers sticking out of the end of a pair of mud-spattered denims with the traditional horizontal rip just under the right buttock.

From buttocks upwards, the body was encased like an Egyptian mummy in a sleeping bag and curled into as near as he could get to the foetal position. The air in the tent had the tang of chemicals mixed with singed hair and fabric from the sleeping bag. The dipstick had crawled inside there to do crack. To say, as we are supposed to say these days, that he was chemically challenged was putting it mildly.

I tucked the torch into my armpit and crawled into the tent to tug the sleeping bag off him, to make sure it was Lee. It didn't occur to me then that he might have suffocated, drowned in his own vomit or burnt his eyebrows off. I knew all three were worth eachway bets.

The sleeping bag came off and I felt and heard a variety of things fall out of it apart from Lee. It was Lee, and he was breathing and when I flashed the torch full face I distinctly saw an eyeball move. Scattered around the floor were the items he'd taken in there with him – there was nothing else in the tent – and I scanned them. Bits of glass from a crushed phial, some strips of metal foil paper, a Zippo lighter, a penknife on a key ring but no key, a stub of a candle and a quartz travelling alarm clock about two inches square. There you had it. A kid not yet old enough to drive crawls into a sleeping bag upside down, inside a dome tent and sets the alarm for seven a.m. before voluntarily parting company with his brain. Freud would have had a field day. Hell's teeth, there could be a PhD in it for me.

Lee's breathing changed. He was probably remembering to exhale. Maybe it was the fresh air and the rain spitting in from the open flap which were reviving him or at least inducing the shivers. He certainly ought to have been shivering, for he was wearing only a T-shirt advertising the band Suede's first CD.

I patted him gently on the cheek.

'Lee. Lee. It's me. Can you hear me?'

I reckoned there was no point in confusing him with tricky details like my name.

I patted both cheeks.

'Lee, can you hear me? I'm looking for Tigger. Lee?'

I shone the torch in his eyes and slapped him.

'Anybody home? Tigger. Where's Tigger?'

He smiled but I think he was smiling at something at the back of his retina, not at me.

'Monster . . . man . . .' he slurred.

'What? Lee, I'm looking for Tigger. Where is he?'

'Monstery . . . man . . . Tigger monster . . .'

'Christ, Lee, straighten out, man. I don't want a character analysis, I want to know where he is. Tigger, remember? Your mate and mine.'

He looked hurt. I must have been getting through. When Vitamin C and methadone programmes fail, try sarcasm.

'I'm telling you. Weekends Tigger goes monstering.'

What the hell does that mean? I wanted to ask, but now I had his attention I had to keep it simple.

'Where, Lee? Where does Tigger go monstering?'

'That's it, monstering.'

He began to scratch his chest with both hands, his nails dragging threads on the cotton T-shirt. He had no idea he was doing it.

'South. In the country. South of the river. Long way. Alarm clock.'

'What?'

'Alarm clock. Whereisit?'

His scratching became louder but he didn't seem to notice. If he hadn't been wearing the T-shirt he would have drawn blood.

'. . . clock . . .' There was panic in the voice now.

I flashed the torch around and picked up his clock for him, holding it to his face. He stopped scratching and took it with both hands.

'Got to sleep,' he said and his eyelids began to droop. He was not faking.

I put my hand on his chest to sit him up again but it was as if I wasn't there. He reached over me and opened the neck of the sleeping bag and made to crawl back inside. I tried to restrain him, to make him comfortable, to settle him, but I

103

admit it must have looked as if I was trying to strangle him. Especially to the couple who were suddenly shining torch beams into the tent.

'Leave him alone, bastard,' said a female voice.

'What do you think you're doing?' added a male voice.

They were the couple from the next tent, the two who had been playing High Risk/Low Risk with a sex manual.

'Get out of there, this minute,' said the woman.

I pulled the peak of my baseball cap down to shield my eyes from their torches which were the lantern type of halogen beam and far more powerful and blinding than mine. Shone upwards they could probably distract aircraft. I edged out of the tent, knee-high to them in a crouch and I heard the metallic clanging sound I had first registered outside their tent. Through the glare of their torches I caught a glimpse of a metal cylinder and I guessed they had armed themselves with the sort of personal fire extinguisher you get as standard issue in big German cars, or you find in mobile homes or, logically enough, on camp sites.

Now there is a lot of bullshit in the movies about what fire extinguishers can do when sprayed into the face and eyes. Water extinguishers and carbon dioxide ones can give you a nasty shock if you're not prepared for it but the smaller ones are more likely to be dry-powder based or contain a chemical cocktail known as BCF. Both those can be highly irritant and cause temporary blindness, and some are popular with second-generation glue-sniffers if a quick spray of butane (cigarette lighter fluid) fails to hit the spot.

But this was not the time to check the small print. I dug my toes into the soft ground for purchase and launched into a run, keeping low. I think it was the woman I hit with my shoulder, but either way one of them grunted as the air went out of them and they slipped and fell backwards.

I wasn't stopping, not even when one of them shouted, 'Hey?' After all, I had offered to stop and chat earlier and they had been positively rude.

Back at Stuart Street I stripped off and soaked in a bath for an hour, which involved getting out twice: once to fiddle the gas meter and get more hot water and once just to make sure that neat tequila was the only thing to drink in the place.

I finished Norman Mailer's *Harlot's Ghost*, which I had been promising to do for a year. (Be honest: two.) It was now so badly damp with bathwater and steam that it could double as a small armchair.

I fed Springsteen, who had appeared through the kitchen window I always left open, twice as silent and far more deadly than any burglar could. I have still to work out how he gets up to the kitchen window from the yard at the back of the house because it's a long, bare drop. But then I try not to worry about things like that. Cats can levitate at will. It's a well-known fact; just nobody's written a law of quantum physics about it yet.

I asked Springsteen if he knew what monstering was. He didn't. Or if he did he wasn't telling. I asked him why Lee wanted an alarm clock and didn't get a straight answer on that either. I asked him how long I ought to string Fenella out over the driving lessons and it was then I realized I'd finished the tequila and had been acting like an idiot.

Springsteen had been asleep for the past half-hour. No wonder he wasn't answering me.

The communal house phone is nailed to the wall by the front door and on the end of a yard of string is an 'honesty book' where we are supposed to log our calls so the bill can be shared out at the end of each quarter. Naturally, I'm very quiet when I use the phone and especially so before seven a.m., which would be a great time for me to make all my calls except nobody I want to phone is conscious then.

Bassotti had said he had an answerphone though, so I could sneak in a call before the house woke up. If I wasn't going to deliver Tigger he wasn't going to hand over any cash, so I would have to turn up for work again, Friday being payday and me now in need of any contribution to the Angel survival fund.

There are answerphone messages and there are answerphone messages and it's a wonder there isn't a university writing course offered on them. There's the laid-back: 'This is the Nineties you know what to do' – BEEP! And there's the pseud, where they play 'Stairway to Heaven' or the theme from *Twin Peaks* before telling you to leave a message, not caring that it's costing the caller God knows how much to listen to it. Then there's the: 'Hermione, Sam, Justin and Frederick are elsewhere at the moment . . .' or the nervous: 'No one here right now but we'll be back very soon so please leave a message,' which is almost invariably left by a single woman living alone who is poised to pick up once she's sure it's not a heavy breather. My favourite belongs to a working girl called Trixie. It really is her name and she does 'give phone' on another line but her main number says: 'Just slipping into something less comfortable. Missing you already,' followed by a battery-powered humming noise rather than a beep.

Bassotti's was dead boring. Just: 'H.B. Builders. Please leave a message for us after the tones,' as if he had read it off the instruction card. He probably had. From what I had seen, he wouldn't have trusted his secretary Kelly to record the message. A pity that; I think she might have enjoyed the challenge.

I took a breath, as you do, and launched into my whining excuses, never having been one to admit to giving up a grand gracefully.

'Mr Bassotti, it's Angel here. You asked me to try and find Tigger for you. Well, no luck so far but I won't give up if you won't. I've found a friend of his and he says he's away for the weekend. Gone monstering, would you believe, which I reckon is some sort of rave party. If you like, I'll . . .' I paused to have a minor heart attack as I heard somebody cough politely just behind my right ear.

It was Mr Goodson from the downstairs flat wearing a woollen dressing gown, pyjamas and slippers. No wonder I hadn't heard him coming. He mouthed something to me. 'What?' I said, then realized I was still talking into the phone.

'Can I get my milk?' he said softly.

I saw that I was leaning up against the front door and all

he wanted was to get his milk in off the step. So the milkman delivered that early. You live and learn.

I moved aside, whispered 'Sorry' and said it again into the phone.

'Sorry about that. Like I said, Tigger's gone off to this monster party out of town but I'll keep looking if your offer's still open. I'll catch you later.'

I hung up and reluctantly made an entry in the honesty book as Mr Goodson was still at my side. Who would have expected him to catch me using the phone even at this time in the morning, let alone on a Friday. He was never seen about the house on Fridays – or any part of the weekend come to think of it.

'Local call,' I said weakly, smiling at him. He rarely looked you in the eye and he wasn't about to start, but it seemed as if he had something he wanted to say.

'I couldn't help but overhear,' he said politely, shuffling his slippers, 'and I certainly didn't mean to.'

I waved a hand in an all-purpose gesture which was meant to say 'think nothing of it' but was probably obscene in several countries.

'It's just that . . .'

'Yes?' I encouraged.

'Well, you said somebody was monstering and you seemed to think it meant going to a party.'

'And it isn't?' I asked gently as if I was in no hurry and, as long as we had an ozone layer, I wasn't.

'No. It's a game.'

'A game? You mean a game show, like *Wheel of Fortune* or something?'

'No, an interactive game.' He began to blush. 'A role-playing game, part physical, part philosophical.'

I looked at him. He went from pink to medium rare. I couldn't think of anything to say all of a sudden.

'You know. Er . . . er . . . fantasy scenarios.' A bizarre thought hit me across the frontal lobes and it must have showed as Mr Goodson's colour deepened to crimson.

'No, er . . . not . . . er . . . It's more the seeking of a quest acted out in a fantasy dimension. The characters require adversaries – monsters.'

'Oh, you mean like *Dungeons and Dragons*?'

'We prefer to call them Adventures in the Nether World.'

'You play?'

'I'm a Grand Vizier. First Class. Level Four,' he said proudly.

Impressed? I was gobsmacked.

10

I was late checking in with Dispatch but I doubted it would damage our working relationship further.

Breakfast with Mr Goodson had been an eye-opener in more ways than one. Not only the juicy details of being a Grand Vizier in the Nether World, but also the chance to have a good snoop around his flat. The fact that people could live without microwaves, VCRs, CDs and still use toast racks and marmalade spoons, was difficult to take in at first but it's still a free world, more or less, and I could make allowances. The Nether World stuff was a piece of cake to take on board after that. Let's face it, even a Mr Goodson has a Dark Side.

Dispatch kept me busy with fiddling little jobs in Soho most of the morning. Two at least could have been done by bikes, avoiding the traffic the way they drive, as they were small parcel deliveries. But it was payday and I had been late so somebody had to suffer and it might as well be me.

I signed myself off for a coffee break just after eleven a.m. and, out of habit, parked on Porter Street. I decided it was a habit I really ought to kick when I saw the Beast there, side-saddle on his bike, chewing on a styrofoam cup.

'Popular dude,' he said for openers. At least I think that's what he said as he still had the coffee carton in his face. When he took it away I could see there were teeth marks around the rim. As in so many other ways, the Beast wasn't equipped with a full set.

'So what's happening?'

'You are in deeee-mand,' he drawled.

'Dispatch?' I asked, knowing it wasn't as I had only just turned off their tinny radio.

'Personal services,' pronounced the Beast, like he'd heard it somewhere else. 'Your customers come to the door these days.'

'Who?'

'Some fat old spick in a red Alfa.'

I felt oddly comforted that our position in any future fraternal united states of Europe seemed assured as long as people like the Beast were about.

'I told him you'd be along. He's waiting round in Old McDonald's for you. Looks the worried type. Sort that has daughters who might well have been boffing. How is your sex life these days, Angel?'

'Like my credit rating: short, uninteresting and not worth paying to have checked out.'

I made sure it was Bassotti by walking by the window twice before going in. He was sitting on a stool balancing an elbow on a ledge just wide enough to double park hamburger cartons. I bought a large black coffee and joined him.

'I got your message,' he said. 'Thought I'd better double check.'

'Double check what?' I realized he was nervous but I could not work out why. It wasn't as if I'd demanded money or anything; well, not recently.

'What you said. You said you reckoned you knew where Tigger was at the weekend.'

'And you came up West on the strength of that?'

He shrugged it off. 'I had business round here. Anyway, like I said, it's worth a few quid and a bit of effort to find that little bleeder. So what you got?'

I saw no harm in telling him.

'There's a chance Tigger's into RLRP – Real Life Role Playing. That's where people dress up and play *Lord of the Rings* and stuff like that.'

I could see I wasn't getting through.

'Look,' I tried, 'just say it's like a weekend retreat where grown men – and women for all I know – run around in some caves playing cowboys and indians, except it's wizards and warlocks and warriors and probably other things beginning with "w" and there's also monsters. And they go on quests and expeditions and the third prize is the Holy Grail or whatever. I'm just telling you what I've been told.'

'And Tigger goes on these things, does he?'

'I think he might work there. They're always looking for people to play the monsters. The paying punters want to be heroes, don't they, struggling against the forces of evil. Nobody wants to have to be the forces of evil, 'specially not if they've paid good money to get there.'

'He works there . . . ?'

'It's a possibility. A friend of his just said he "went monstering" at weekends. These role playing games require monsters – well, somebody to play monsters – and a guy I know assures me that there's only one place open Friday, Saturday and Sunday and that's down in Surrey. Which would tie in with what Tigger's friend told me, that he was doing it south of here. I'd assumed south of the river, but maybe he meant south of London.'

'What sort of a place are we talking about here?' Bassotti still wasn't sure this was kosher.

'A place called Nether World, and it's run from some caves in a place called Badger's Bottom. I was saving that till last, just in case you didn't believe the other stuff. It does exist, really. It's off the M25, not far from Biggin Hill. You know, the old wartime airfield.'

Even I thought this was beginning to sound like a con. Bassotti wasn't old enough to remember the war either. And if he had been, which side would he have been on?

'So we're talking running around in fields here, are we?' he tried, his mind wandering as much as mine was starting to.

'No, it's all done underground. There's some caves, natural ones. You know, holes in the side of a big bit of ground. During the war they were enlarged to be used as air raid shelters and places for stashing files and things. They go on for miles they say. You could get a coupla hundred people in there . . . if you stack 'em right . . .' I ended lamely.

Bassotti rubbed his chin thoughtfully. Then he glanced around before putting his hand in his pocket and producing a roll of notes. If he had wanted to look any more suspicious I suppose he could have taken his trousers down and balanced a hand grenade on his dick, but it would have been close.

'Go down there and have a look around, will you? You're the expert, you'll find him. Tell him to come and see me, OK?'

He began to rub the wad of notes with his thumb, like a magician gearing up for a card trick. I was happy to be hypnotized.

'I'm only guessing he's there,' I said coyly, trying to work out if the notes were twenties or not. Before they changed the colour strip, it was difficult to tell under fluorescent light from even a foot away. 'It could be a wasted trip.'

'I'm a builder, I pay people to waste time,' he said, but he wasn't joking. 'And, anyway, you know where it is.'

That wasn't strictly true, though I could easily find out. But if I gave him a road map and a set of directions, he wouldn't need me and there would be no 'finder's fee'.

'Look, if you're willing to pay for my time and my gas, I'll pop down there tomorrow and mingle.'

He shook his head.

'Not tomorrow, today. This afternoon.'

'Ah, slight problemette there. You see I have this problem called work. Like I'm at it, now, and if you don't show they get really unreasonable and don't pay you.'

'They'd pay you if you were on a job?'

'Sure.'

'Then I'll ring them and book you to take me to ... where's good?'

'Brighton? That's usually good for an afternoon job, and I bet that's been said more than once before now.'

He didn't get it or he wasn't listening.

'OK, we'll say you have to come out to the office, pick somebody up and take them to Brighton. By the time you get back, that's your afternoon accounted for, right?'

'If you're picking up the bill, yeah. This finding Tigger is getting to be a big deal with you, isn't it?'

'You don't know the half,' he said.

He rubbed the roll of notes some more and peeled a few off but he wasn't so much counting them as using them to mop the sweat from his hands.

*

I found a phone box on Baker Street and rang the house. The only person who should have been home at that time was Mr Goodson, and it was.

'Great, you haven't left yet.' Sometimes I think I should get prizes for stating the bleeding obvious.

'I was about to. My train leaves at . . .'

'How does the Grand Vizier fancy arriving in Nether World by taxi?'

Mr Goodson talked more on the ride down to Surrey than I had ever heard before and he'd been living at Stuart Street when I moved in. Maybe he was conscious of going for some personal record himself, for he kept stopping and saying things like 'Oh dear, I am going on, aren't I?' He was, but I didn't stop him. It was a useful briefing.

He had been visiting Nether World for four years or so as and when he could afford it. Normally this meant day-trips on Saturdays or Sundays but occasionally, like now, he flexed his flexi-time schedule at the local government office and took a Friday off so he could stay the weekend. (Local bed and breakfast. Mr and Mrs Lambert. Very reasonable. You get sausages with breakfast.)

You got a game card every time you played, he explained, and he was up to Level Four, first class, as the points had mounted up.

'What do you get points for?'

'Inflicting damage, damage limitation to your game role character and bonus ones for the amount of treasure or trophy returned from a quest.'

And I had to ask.

'This damage business. Sounds a bit violent.'

'It's not, really, though some of the monsters go over the top sometimes. Some of them can't, of course. Zombies are supposed to be the slowest of the Undead and you can always hear them coming.' (I bit my tongue and said nothing.) 'And the Skeletons move quick but are relatively weak. The Vampires are powerful but can be defeated by spells. The ones to watch out for are the Ghouls. They're sneaky and powerful and fast. Very tricky – they play dumb and pretend they can't understand the Spell of Warding.'

I put money on Tigger being a Ghoul if he was there.

'And just what do these characters do . . . er . . . ?' I tailed off because I couldn't go on calling him Mr Goodson now he was sitting in the back of Armstrong and I was picking his brains, but I was damned if I could remember his first name, assuming I'd ever been told it.

He didn't notice, because he was on his pet subject, which just proves what I always say: ask the right question and you can get anyone to tell you anything (Rule of Life No. 83).

'Their role is to stop the questors and the valiant from reaching their goal, or at least slow them down and soak up their life-force.'

'You have life-force?' I asked like other people swap brands of deodorant.

'Every game player is allocated a life-force. Combat damage' – there was that word again – 'and hostile spells can all diminish your life-force value. The more points you retain, the more you carry over into the next game, then the next level and so onwards.'

'Sounds like life, really. And you've got to Grand Vizier level?'

I was watching him in the mirror. He was serious about all this.

'Yes, and that's my game name as well. You'll need one too if you're coming into the caves.'

'Game name?'

I flashed my lights to overtake a Fiat Panda driven at twenty-two m.p.h. by a large blue hat which I guessed had a little old lady somewhere under it. A few names sprang to mind.

'Oh yes, no one uses their real names in Nether World.'

Which probably cut down on the insurance claims, I thought.

'The younger fraternity,' Mr Goodson went on, 'go for names like Simeon or Ragnor or Hakklon. There's a very competent Warrior Priest at my level who goes by the game name Schmeichel. That sounds Dutch to me.'

It was Danish and I didn't want to spoil it by telling him it was the name of the Manchester United goalkeeper.

'The thing to remember is not to go for anything from Tolkien. It's frowned upon as frivolous.'

'But why will I need a game name? Can't I just ask backstage or something? I just want to see if Tigger's here or not.' Besides, I'd left my wand and fairy dust at home.

'It doesn't work like that. No one gets passed by the Gatekeeper unless they are playing and the monsters have to be there before the game players turn up. They have to get into costume, pick a route and then lie in ambush. Sometimes the monsters have to play two or three quests at the same time. So few people want to be monsters these days, they're quite in demand.'

I wouldn't have said that, but it was neither the time nor the place for a philosophical argument.

As I pulled Armstrong into the muddy field which served as the car park for Nether World, I realized I had done one thing right that morning when I had put on a black T-shirt. It seemed to be the uniform for everyone around the cars and the entrance, which was marked by a sign saying: 'The Real World Declines From Hereon In'.

In fact, I hadn't seen so much long hair or so many black T-shirts since the Black Sabbath collection came out on video.

It had been easy enough to find, despite Mr Goodson trying to give directions from the back. I hoped his sense of geography improved once he was underground. The road sign indicating Biggin Hill and Badger's Bottom had been added to in spray paint so that it ended: 'Nether World ½ mile further'. It read like the instructions on an elevator to hell.

Mr Goodson climbed out of the driver's-side door and put a small suitcase and a duffel bag down on the ground.

'I'll leave my overnight things with the Gatekeeper,' he said. 'You'll want to get off once you find your friend, and my bed and breakfast place is just a few minutes' walk into the village. But I'll get changed here, if you don't mind. I like to make an entrance.'

'Feel free,' I said. He left the duffel bag on the ground and took the suitcase with him as he climbed back into Armstrong.

There were more people milling around than I had expected and something like fifty cars in the field. The entrance to the caves was sheltered by some small trees, probably planted by the local council to try and hide the goings-on in there. And with good reason, judging by some of the people coming out after a hard day in the Nether World.

Virtually everyone was wearing make-up, almost entirely black or dark green, though one or two had taken a bit of trouble and added sparkly gold eye-shadow. Black T-shirts and jeans were the order of the day, but whereas mine advertised a garage and spray-joint in Raleigh, North Carolina, most of the ones coming up from the underworld were adorned with gold or silver stick-on stars or pentacles or crescent moons. Then came a group wearing armour. Home-made breastplates and leg guards, probably cardboard but painted shiny silver and convincing enough from a distance. I spotted two guys with horned Viking helmets on their heads, one of them carrying a large double-headed battle-axe. It would have been more convincing had he not been swinging it one-handed like a golf club, giving away the fact that it was polystyrene. But still, I could understand why the residents of Badger's Bottom didn't especially want to run into them on a dark night.

'You'll be given a weapon from the armoury,' said Mr Goodson from the back of Armstrong, 'but some people like to make their own.'

'Fine. Is there much light down there?'

'None at all. Lanterns are permitted but if you take a torch, you have to keep it pointed upwards so the effect is like candlelight. Most of us don't bother. The Game Guide has a torch of course.'

'Game Guide?'

'He's a sort of referee. He directs your quest and calls for Time Freezers when you can alter the action or assess your level of damage.'

There he went, talking about damage again. I walked round to the back of Armstrong and opened the boot. I found my torch, checked it worked again and slid it into my jeans in the small of my back, pulling my T-shirt out loose over it. I locked my jacket in the boot after taking out some of Bassotti's money. I shivered in the cool afternoon breeze but I worked on the basis that it was better to leave everything valuable in the real world. I was entering Nether World with just the bare essentials: my car keys.

The thought struck me that if Tigger was in monster gear (and the people I'd seen so far were the paying punters, so God knew what the monsters looked like), he might recognize me before I spotted him. My problem was I was badly underdressed.

I looked in the glove compartment where I stash things as and when I can be bothered. I found an ageing packet of Piccadilly No.1 cigarettes and a Zippo lighter (repro, but good repro) and something I had just thought of, the single black nylon stocking. I smiled as I suddenly remembered the circumstances which had led to it getting there in the first place, then frowned as I remembered the reasons why it was impossible to return it to its owner. Still, one woman's loss was my gain.

I lit a cigarette with the Zippo and took a deep draw, revelling in the political incorrectness of it. Then I pulled the stocking taut over my left fist and took a guess at where two eye-holes should go. I blew on the tip of the cigarette and dabbed two holes, enlarging them with my finger. I measured it up against my face and it seemed to fit, so I dropped the Zippo into the toe of the stocking and tied a knot to keep it there, then pulled the stocking over my head. In Armstrong's wing mirror, I looked like a pigtailed bank robber.

I thought it wasn't bad for on-the-spot improvisation or at least I did until I tried to smoke the rest of the cigarette. If nothing else I had discovered another good way of giving up: try inhaling through an old black 15-denier. Filter tips? Who needs 'em?

'I'm ready,' came a voice from the other side of the cab.

I don't know which of us was the more surprised.

Facing each other over the bonnet, there was I, my features distorted modelling ski masks for serial killers.

But on the other side was Mr Goodson in a full length

crimson cloak covered in runic letters. His face was streaked with green and black face-paint zigzags and around his neck was an amulet which on closer inspection was a life-size metal frog, the sort you can buy in garden shops to enhance your garden pond. On his head, adding two feet to his height, was a coned wizard's hat, obviously hand-stitched from patches of black leather with loving care. So that's what he did at weekends.

'Er . . . fine,' I mumbled through the stocking.

'I see you're getting into the spirit of things.' He smiled, genuinely pleased.

'Yeah. Let's go to work, shall we?'

On the way into the caves there was a sign saying: 'Real World Currency does NOT exist Beyond the Armoury'. Underneath that was an exchange rate should you wish to buy anything in the Nether World where everything was given as equivalent ducats or doubloons. If I had had a stockbroker I would have rung him and told him that in Nether World the Deutschmark was having a bitch of a time against the doubloon.

The actual entrance to the caves was a long slope down into the dark, starting off as grass then moving through gravel to the smooth, dry rock. They had spaced the lights out at increasing intervals so that your eyes got used to the gloom. Either that or they were really cutting back on the electricity bills.

The first barrier was a trestle table behind which sat a huge bearded guy with forearms the like of which I hadn't seen outside a butcher's. He was wearing a Mettallica T-shirt and looked like a hundred other roadies I knew who had lived too long on fried food. Mr Goodson told me, with some reverence, that he was the Gatekeeper.

Whatever other qualities he had, the Gatekeeper needed a calculator to work out two tickets at twelve pounds each. Then when Mr Goodson showed him a card, he made a great play of stamping it with a wizened bit of inky rubber and said, 'Welcome, Grand Vizier.'

'My friend is a novice,' said Mr Goodson and I gave him a killer look from behind my stocking mask.

'Then you'll need a game card,' said the Gatekeeper.

He produced a Filofax from below the table and found a blank one between the pages. It took him a while to find a pen and then he wrote 'Initiate' on the cover, folded the card to the size of a European driving licence and began to hand it over.

'Follow the signs for Level One. Someone will explain the weapons and damage system. Keep your card with you during the game. Oh, wait, you need a game name and a Character Alignment.'

'A what?'

'Alignment,' he said wearily. 'Are you Lawful or Chaotic?'

'Lawful, every time. Yes, put me down for some of that.'

'And Character?'

I hesitated as I always do over trick questions. Mr Goodson helped me out.

'You can't be a Wizard on your first game, so you must choose one of the other Character classes.'

'Which are?'

'Warrior – they do most of the fighting.'

'Not me, I think.'

'Priest – they're usually in the thick of the fighting, casting spells.'

'Perhaps something quieter?'

'Archer? Scout? Pathfinder? Caveman? They're usually regarded as expendable.'

'Anything sort of further back towards the rear?'

'Warrior Priest? They actually do most of the healing and can heal their own wounds too, with simple spells.'

'Warrior Priest, eh? A sort of aggressive clergyman – but mildly aggressive? Yeah, I could go for that.'

'Fine,' said the Gatekeeper heavily. 'Warrior Priest it is. And what's your game name?'

'BBW,' I said. 'Just the initials. Is that OK?'

'Call yourself BMW for all I care,' said the Gatekeeper, which I thought was no way to talk to a man of the cloth.

11

'Roll call for Quest Four,' said the Game Guide producing a small notepad from the folds of his robes. 'Grand Vizier, Pan, Heartbreaker, Skullsplitter – thought that was a beer – Ug, Bindweed, Bog Myrtle – looks like we've got the Greens in today – Simeon, BBW – is that right? – Canticle – oh, hello there, Kirstie, didn't recognize you for the minute, when did you have the hair blued? – Athelstan and Doric. All here? Good. Any Novitiates?'

Nobody moved. Mr Goodson nudged me in the ribs and mouthed 'You' at me.

'No, I don't do drugs,' I whispered.

'Anyone not played before?' asked the Game Guide in a sarcastic drawl which his parents had paid dearly for through a private education.

'Sorry, me,' I said, stepping forward.

He gave me the once over, stocking mask and all, and I could almost hear him thinking. He shook his head resignedly and yelled: 'Armourer!'

A straight-looking guy in Levis and a commando pullover appeared from round the corner of the tunnel in which we were lined up. He was carrying an armful of plastic weapons ranging from clubs and swords to battle-axes and the scimitar-style sword with the nick in the blade which I know is called a seax because I play Trivial Pursuit for money.

'Come with me.' He jerked his head and I followed him around the tunnel.

He dropped his bundle of weapons on the rock floor near the wall of the cave, which was now as smooth as marble and icy to the touch.

'Character?'

'Warrior Priest,' I answered proudly.

'Then you shouldn't see the thick of the action, but you have a duty to defend yourself.' He sized me up. 'Going to wear armour?'

'Hadn't thought about it,' I said honestly.

'Best you don't. The Ghouls might mistake you for a Warrior. The Vampires are best dealt with by spells and you're lucky, you have a Grand Vizier on your quest. But you'll need something for the Zombies and the Skeletons. Sword or club?'

'I'm more of a sword person.'

He looked me over for tell-tale signs of not taking this seriously, but fortunately I had the mask on.

'Now I have to say this, I only hope you listen.' He picked up a plastic sword and wielded it violently against the wall of the cave. I flinched. 'There. It might be plastic, but it can still hurt. So you have to pull your strokes, always. If you hit something and it howls, that's acting. If it screams, you're getting carried away.'

'What if it doesn't say anything?'

'Then you're probably hitting the wall. If you are struck on the extremities, arms or legs, you can continue to fight, but body and head wounds require assistance from a spell-binder. You're a Warrior Priest, though, right?'

'Yeah.'

'Then you can heal yourself as well as others. Do you know the spell of healing?'

'Not really.'

' "I abjure thee vile spirit and bid you gone from these mortal places, binding and rebinding flesh to whole again." It's a bit of a mouthful, so try it.'

I did.

'Not bad,' said the Armourer, 'but it's "vile" spirit, not "blithe".'

'Sorry.'

'Now get back to your quest group. The Game Guide will be issuing the challenge.'

'Can I just ask one thing?' He nodded as he bent to pick up the spare weaponry. 'I was due to meet a mate of mine after the . . . the . . . afterwards. He's monstering I think. Where would he be?'

'In place, waiting to ambush you. You'll probably run into him. We've only got four monsters on this afternoon, so they're working double quests. It's like double shifts.'

I wondered if they had a union.

'Thanks. My mate is called Tigger. Is he on today?'

'Chopsy little git, can't stand still?'

'Got him in one.'

'Yeah, he's around somewhere. He'll probably find you before you find him.'

'I was afraid of that.'

I picked up the plastic sword he had selected for me and, resting the blade on my shoulder, rejoined my group.

The Game Guide was dressed like a monk except instead of sandals he wore Travel Fox trainers which had reflectors built into the heels. I supposed they came in useful down in Nether World. He pulled up the cowl of his robe and addressed us.

'You are a gathering of mercenaries all returned from various wars and here' – he waved his arms – 'in this tavern at a crossroads by chance. You are wary of each other at first but you have one thing in common. You all seek further action. I am a traveller who comes to this tavern and I have gold enough for drink and meat.'

He waved his arms again and the group arranged themselves as if around a large rectangular table, crouching or sitting on the cold rock floor. I clocked them for the first time. Mr Goodson (sorry, Grand Vizier) was way the oldest, and I had a nasty feeling I was close on being the next.

Pan, Skullsplitter, Athelstan and Simeon were obviously Warriors and raring to go. They were miming drinking beer by the stone jug better than the average Glasgow pub crowd on a Friday night. Ug was a caveman – the club and fur leotard gave that away. God knows what the rest were. Canticle was the only obvious female, but then the light was bad.

One of them offered to 'fill my bowl', which would have led to a fight in some of the places I go, but I played along.

We must have looked like a dress rehearsal for *The Student Prince* (with a director on speed) from a distance.

'You have refreshed yourself enough!' announced the Game Guide, which I thought was a bit rich as I was still on my first pint.

'Now you must decide. Is it to be a Quest? Or must I hire your services as bodyguards for my Adventure?'

There was some dissension in the ranks here, but it was fairly half-hearted. Dammit, they'd paid for a Quest and they were going to get one.

'What's the difference?' I hissed at the Grand Vizier.

'A Quest means there will be treasure hidden along the way and we can share in the profits,' said Mr Goodson out loud.

'Then we get adventure and profit!' shouted one of the Warriors; Simeon, I think. They all looked alike after a few stone jugs of ale.

'We are agreed?' asked one of the Warriors; Skullsplitter maybe. He brandished a home-made double-headed battle-axe and put on a ferocious expression which almost took my mind off his acne.

'Agreed,' we all muttered, nobody wanting to argue with a skin condition like that.

'Then the journey will be long and hard with many dangers,' said the Game Guide.

'Many dangers,' muttered Bindweed and Bog Myrtle in unison.

'There is a Princess held in the depths of Nether World by the spells of the Undead who have combined forces to denude her of her powers and her treasure.'

'Her treasure,' said two or three of them in chorus.

'Denude her,' I said, too late and too loud. They glared at me.

'Along the way we fight for and reclaim her three magic torcs,' the Game Guide went on. He was getting into his stride now.

'Three torcs,' came the echo. They were lapping it up.

'With all three, the Vampires guarding her will be powerless to resist us. With less than three, we will have to fight for her.'

'Fight for her.' They were on their feet at this.

'Then follow me! The Quest begins!'

'The Quest!' they cheered.

'No chance of one for the road?' I asked, looking down at my imaginary ale. But I was talking to myself and had to jog to catch them up.

The first ambush caught us about five hundred yards into the tunnel complex, not that I knew much about it. The Game Guide and one or two others had small pencil torches which they shone at the roof so there was virtually total darkness ahead and underfoot. Suddenly there were two characters wearing what felt and smelled like old sacks in among us, waving their arms around like windmills.

Utter confusion reigned among our gallant band of mercenaries. The Grand Vizier shouted for his spell-pouch, which he had dropped. ('Stolen by elves!' somebody yelled. 'No, I really have dropped it,' said Mr Goodson.) Skullsplitter yelled for more room in which to swing his broadsword, at least we assumed he meant his broadsword. Canticle screamed and screamed and Simeon staggered back into me clutching his arm and moaning something about being wounded to the quick by a venom-coated blade.

It appeared from the way he was clinging to me that he wanted me to do something about it.

'Go on, then, heal me.'

'Pardon?'

'You're a Warrior Priest aren't you? Say the spell of healing.'

I did my best, but he got up and walked off in disgust, muttering that he would just have to lose life-force and, anyway, it was 'vile spirit' I was supposed to say.

The panic subsided and the Ghouls or Zombies or whatever they had been disappeared. The Game Guide put his torch on full, aimed at a section of the wall and yelled: 'Time Out.'

If I was expecting a cup of tea and biscuits I was way out of line. A Time Out involved standing in a line against the cave wall as the Game Guide produced his notebook. While he was doing this, I screwed up my eyes and tried to work out where the entrance to the caves lay and I realized I hadn't a clue. We had taken so many turns that I was totally disorientated. I seemed to be the only one who minded.

'Well, my fine band of mercenaries, that was a shambles, wasn't it? We'll now do a life-force reckoning and you must be honest. Remember, I witnessed the swath those Skeletons cut through you. I'm working on a fifty per cent damage ratio. First off, though, any fatalities?'

Now there was a daft question, but I half expected it to get an answer.

'Very well, I'll let that one pass,' he said. 'Now, sound off. Skullsplitter?'

'No hits, one Skeleton kill.'

'Nice try,' said the Game Guide. 'I'll give you the no hits. Athelstan?'

'Non-venomous wound to left side body part, healed by Grand Vizier.'

'Good. One tenth magic potency reduction to Grand Vizier. Bog Myrtle?'

And so he went on down the line until even I got the general idea.

'BBC? Sorry, BBW. Is that right?'

'Yes. No hits, no spells.'

'Not too impressive for a Warrior Priest, is it?' he smirked before he went on to Bindweed. What did he want? Blood?

When he had finished his list, he put the notebook away and shone his pencil torch up under his chin.

'Now listen. This company of Warriors has reached only the edge of the Dark One's sphere of power. From here on we will face greater dangers as our foes grow stronger. They will tempt us with false clues and send stronger opponents. We must be on our guard. Is the company ready to proceed?'

The Mild Bunch muttered that it was and then Ug, the caveman character, stepped forward and pointed at his chest then towards the dark tunnel ahead.

'Ug, Ug, Ug,' he said.

'Brave lowlife,' said the Game Guide, 'the honour is yours.'

'What's going on?' I whispered to Canticle, whom I had decided to stay behind in case she fell.

'Ug is volunteering to scout ahead of the company,' she enthused, almost dewy-eyed with hero-worship.

'Why doesn't he say so?' I had to ask.

'Cavemen are only allowed one line of dialogue.'

Of course. Silly me.

Fifty yards further in, or it could have been a hundred, it was getting impossible to tell, we came across our next challenge. I was only surprised that no one had said, 'It's quiet; too quiet.'

Three planks of wood about six feet long were laid out on the floor. Beyond them was a semi-circular cave carved out of the main tunnel and this was lit by two red-filtered lanterns. Chained to the far wall was a woman old enough to know better in a white shroud, her head bent on to her chest and one of the worst-fitting long black wigs I had ever seen cascading hair almost to the floor. In front of her, carrying plastic swords, were two more monsters, covered from head to toe in black sacking and moaning the way football fans do at referees.

Ug, our kamikaze caveman, strode on to the planks of wood and, yelling his one line of dialogue, offered battle to the Zombies.

They creamed him. Working together, they rained blows down on him until he staggered back into the arms of the Grand Vizier, amidst a howling of protest, obscenities and spells from our side. One of the Zombies, a big thickset guy, made a triumphant gesture with his fist. He reminded me of one of the stewards I knew at the last Guns N' Roses concert.

'A plan! We need a plan!' went up the cry from the gallant mercenaries.

As they got into a huddle to decide tactics, I stepped forward to get a better look at the Zombies, but both were too big for Tigger.

A torch came on in my face.

'Excuse me, old chap,' said the Game Guide drily. 'It's BBW, isn't it? Yes, I thought so. Don't want to worry you but you've just stepped into a mile-deep chasm at the bottom of which are the Quicksands of the Grey Worm.'

I looked down at the tunnel floor and then realized that everyone else was treating the three planks as a bridge. I hopped back on and whispered, 'Sorry.'

'Do try and keep up,' said the Game Guide before flicking off his torch and disappearing into the gloom again.

There followed a good half-hour's debate about whether we should rush the bridge or blind the Zombies and free the bird with magic. I was told to drag the fatally wounded Ug out of the action and to heal him. As I did so, trying to remember the spell, he said, 'Take your time, mate, I've done my bit,' and produced half a cigarette from somewhere inside his furs.

'Got a light, mate?' he whispered.

'As a matter of fact, yes,' I said, peeling off my stocking mask and fumbling out the Zippo.

'Cheers,' he said, drawing deeply. 'Want a pull?'

I could tell from the smell it was the sharing sort of cigarette.

'Don't they mind?' I asked.

'Nah. Most of 'em are reconstructed hippies round here and the punters are either civil servants or kids who think it's magical, herbal tobacco.'

I passed back the joint and asked him if he came here often.

'Only to keep my daughter amused. She's the one called Canticle. It keeps her off the streets.'

I marvelled at the fact that he was old enough to have a daughter as big as Canticle. It must be a sign of getting older when even the cavemen appear younger.

Eventually the Grand Vizier spell-gunned the chained-up woman and got her to reveal she was in fact a Vampire luring us into the red glow. This by all accounts was as potentially damaging as the red glow Ug and I were getting. Anyway, then the Zombies rushed the bridge and there was an almighty punch-up which the Game Guide had to halt by calling Time Out.

Once again we were lined up against the wall while he

checked off our wounds, use of spells and all that other stuff.

When he got to me, he paused.

'BBW? Wait, I have to ask, though I know I'll regret it. What the fuck does BBW stand for?'

'Bishop of Bath and Wells,' I said honestly.

'This is the labyrinth of Kraal,' said the Game Guide.

No it wasn't. It was half a dozen tea-chests with their bottoms knocked out stacked to look like a honeycomb. But I didn't say anything.

'Only one of these tunnels is unguarded by the Vampire of Kraal, whose single glance is enough to blind a mortal. You will need volunteers to establish which is the safe tunnel.'

That sparked off another committee meeting and although Skullsplitter had been acting like he was our leader for most of the Quest, he wasn't too keen to go first. I whispered to Canticle that I couldn't see the problem. So they got blinded; I could heal them. If I remembered the spell.

'Only a magician at the level of the Grand Vizier can heal blindness,' she said in her don't-you-know-anything voice. 'And he is using up his magic too quickly. He will not have the strength to carry on if he has to heal five cases of blindness.'

'Bit like the National Health Service, really, isn't it?' I tried jovially, but she was taking it far too seriously. Why couldn't some kids be more like their parents?

Then someone volunteered to be first; Doric or Pan, I was past caring which. They advanced cautiously towards the honeycomb, chose a box and began to crawl in. There was an instantaneous blood-curdling scream and whoever it was came out fast with all engines on reverse Warp Drive, staggering about and screaming quite realistically.

At first I thought something dreadful had happened, then I realized that the green jelly dripping from Pan or Doric's face was nothing more than that, green joke-shop gunk.

'Let me risk the Vampire!' yelled Simeon, charging forward.

'Brave Simeon!' they all shouted, not giving a toss about

poor Pan/Doric who really was blundering into the wall trying to get the green jelly out of his eyes.

Simeon got the same treatment with the box he chose and, from the sound of things, a couple of whacks with a plastic sword. This time the scream was one of triumph and it came from behind the boxes. If I could have put money on it, I would have bet this was the one Vampire I knew socially.

I pulled the torch out of the back of my jeans and held it at my side, transferring my sword to my left hand.

'Let me take up the challenge!' I shouted, partly to drown out Simeon who was wiping his face with both hands and asking if anyone had a Kleenex.

'Let . . . B . . . B . . . BBW . . . take up the challenge!' they all yelled after an initial hesitation.

A hand came down on my shoulder. It was the Grand Vizier.

'Angel, are you sure you know what you're doing?'

'Are frogs waterproof, Grand Vizier? Can't stop, got a meet with a Vampire.'

I selected one column of the boxes where three were piled on top of each other and ran towards it. About ten feet away, I turned the torch on and held it out in front of me, aiming at the top box. I caught a glimpse of a white face before I threw the torch into the top box, ducked and started to crawl through the bottom one.

'Put that fucking light out!' I heard someone curse and there was more than one cry of 'That's cheating' from behind me.

I got my shoulders through the bottom box and as the torch was still bouncing light all around, I could quite clearly see a pair of legs wearing black tracksuit trousers in front of me. I put my arms around them and the Vampire of Kraal went arse over tip back against the wall.

I crawled out and recovered my torch and shone it down.

The Vampire was holding his head and moaning. He had dropped a large plastic catapult with an enlarged sling designed to fire great blobs of jello gunk and at his side was a bucket of the stuff.

'Hello, Tigger,' I said. 'Fancy knocking off early for a pint? I wanted a word as it happens.'

When he heard my voice, it clicked. With the stocking over my head he'd had no idea who had whipped his legs from under him.

'Angel? Is that you? Shit, I might have known.'

I offered him a hand to help pull him to his feet, not knowing that the real monsters were waiting for us in the outside world.

12

'The Vampire of Kraal accepts your sacrifice!' yelled Tigger, switching off my torch and handing it down to me. Then, under his breath, he said: 'Come on, we can piss off the back way.'

Behind us, at the entrance to the Vampire's cave, the jolly questors sounded to be turning on each other.

'A sacrifice! BBW has been sacrificed!'

'Bollocks. That's not in the rule book.'

'Of all the Undead, the Vampire can transcend the mortal laws.'

'Not at Level Four it naffin' can't. Who's got the *Guide to Nether World*?'

'Will the Vampire take ransom so we can buy BBW back?'

'This isn't the fucking *Crystal Maze* you know.'

'Time Out! Time Out!' The Game Guide brought them to order.

By then Tigger and I were round a corner, him leading, me following blindly. But not totally blindly. There was some light here and it took me a minute or two to work out that it was coming from Tigger himself. The rugby shirt or whatever it was he was wearing had been decorated with luminous paint, mostly with stars and pentangles to match those on his cheeks in some sort of luminous make-up. He would probably have registered on a geiger counter.

'How did you find me down here?' Tigger asked, keeping his voice down.

'Lee sort of indicated you used the Underground but I thought he meant the Circle Line, not this.'

He was still walking just ahead of me, far surer of his footing than I was on the uneven surface of the cave.

131

'Usually, he can't remember what day it is, but I don't tell him much for his own good. He'll blab to anyone. Was he flashing any cash about?'

'Not when I saw him,' I said truthfully.

He shot a look at me which I had to take seriously, despite his make-up.

'You didn't hurt him did you?'

That threw me for a minute.

'Of course not. Why should I? He'd no idea where you were. He mentioned that you went monstering and I just happened to run into someone who knew the scene down here. That's the way it happened.'

He put his head down and walked on. The rock floor inclined upwards now and there was a cool breeze in our faces. There was also much more light here, though I kept my torch on and pointed at the ground just in front of us.

'You haven't asked me why I came to find you,' I said. 'Or did you have me down for a weekend Vampire hunter all along?'

He snorted a sort of half-laugh.

'I was always worried about Lee. Like I said, he's a blabber. That's why I kept him out of it as much as I could. He never even asked where the money was coming from. Probably wouldn't have been able to handle it anyway, not all the others. He's quite loyal in his own little way.'

Out of it? Out of what? What money?

'But I didn't think they'd send you, Angel. Good move, though, with us on the same wavelength, so to speak.'

'Tigger, what are you droning on about?' I snapped. 'All I'm doing is delivering a message for Bert Bassotti.'

'Oh yeah? That's all, is it? What, it's my birthday suddenly?'

I took a deep breath. Negotiating with the Vampire of Kraal had made sense compared to this. 'Look, Bert just wants his van back. Tell me where it is and give me the keys and I'll deliver it. No more hassle. OK?'

'And you think . . .' He paused. 'Listen.'

'I can't hear anything.'

Then I did. Someone shouting: 'Begone from our path vile spirits . . .' Or similar.

'It's the next Quest. They're ahead of schedule,' hissed Tigger. 'Come on, your chance to be a monster.'

Before I could say anything, he grabbed the plastic sword I had been carrying and disappeared. I fumbled the torch to catch a glimpse of his trainers rounding the corner up ahead. I followed, keeping the beam of the torch pointed down at my feet.

'Surprise attack!' someone yelled. 'Warriors to the fore! Zombies!' I realized it was Tigger's voice.

Around the corner, the tunnel seemed packed with heaving, screaming bodies. A couple of gamesters had torches, thin pencil-beam ones and they were waving erratically like the special effects for a Darth Vader sword fight.

I flicked my torch off so I could follow Tigger by his luminous shirt. He seemed to be laying about him with gusto, swinging the sword and carving a path through the unwitting role players who were trying to respond as if this had been what they had paid for all along. Once he got through them he'd be away on his toes and I'd never find him. I was pretty sure I couldn't find the exit without him. What I really needed was a pair of those infra-red goggles which are standard issue to serial killers these days. I did the next best thing and put my head down and charged.

I was doing quite well getting through the ruck when I was jumped by a caveman. I knew it was a caveman because he had a big plastic club and he shouted 'Ug!' a lot. Constantly, in fact.

He got quite excited when his first blow sent me staggering into the cave wall and then I guess I must have tripped over my own feet because suddenly I was on my knees and he was standing in front of me, raining blows down on my back.

I think it wasn't so much his obvious pleasure in taking his frustrations out on the Undead (a much maligned minority group) as his constant 'Ug! Ug! Ug!' chant of victory that finally made me lose my temper. I mean the guy's conversation was minimal, bogus and probably sad. So I brought the torch up between his legs and I was up and running before his plastic club hit the ground.

A very confused Game Guide was shouting 'Time Out!' to calm things down, but I was through them and round another corner I turned the torch on. The tunnel stretched twenty yards in front of me but there was no sign of Tigger. There was his shirt though, which he'd abandoned, along with the plastic sword.

I jogged on, reasoning that the new group must have come in this way so may be the entrance wasn't far. Fifty yards further and I risked turning off the torch. There was enough light for me to realize I was in the area where we had first assembled, pretending to be mercenaries drinking at the Last Chance saloon. I wondered if the bar was still open.

There were figures up ahead in the tunnel who looked as if they'd already had a few drinks from the way they were bouncing off the walls. Then I realized that only one of them was bouncing – or rather, being bounced.

I flattened myself against the right-hand wall of the tunnel. As I got nearer I could hear what they were saying almost as clearly as I could hear the fleshy thumps as Tigger was slammed repeatedly into the rock.

'. . . right nice of you to run straight into our arms, that was. Bleedin' 'ell, we could've spent a month down 'ere looking for you.'

There was another thump and a cry as Tigger ricocheted off the wall and into a fist. He doubled up, but managed a 'Go fuck yourself' before sinking to his knees.

Even in the gloom I could sense that the one who was laying into Tigger was enjoying his work. The other, bigger, one stood a step away.

'No marks, Sammy,' he said. 'Mr Hubbard told us not to mark 'im.'

'Then let's get 'im up and out of this rat hole. These weirdos give me the creeps.'

The big one stooped over Tigger and pulled him upright, by the hair judging from Tigger's squealing. I was so close now I could have banged their heads together, but these didn't strike me as off-duty civil servants playing at cavemen. These were the genuine article.

'Excuse me, are you part of Quest Four?' I said loudly to curb the tremble in my voice as I switched the torch on them. 'You have to keep up with the others or you'll lose points from your game card.'

Almost instantly I knew it wasn't going to work.

The bigger one said 'Shit!' and flung up an arm to shield his eyes. The smaller one squinted and looked down but I saw enough of his weasel profile to know I'd seen him before. He was the Sammy who had been driving the JCB in Bassotti's yard.

'Do 'im,' said Sammy and I realized he was talking about me.

But realizing it didn't help avoid it.

Something swished through the air and I can't say I remembered feeling it hit me in the side of the face so much as wondering why my head had apparently left my body. Then I wasn't thinking much about anything. I was just rolling on the ground; ground which I knew to be solid rock but which suddenly felt like the North Atlantic. My whole universe was swelling and rolling like I was bouncing on a giant, cold water bed. I was going to throw up. I was going to try and throw up through a nylon stocking. But I must have done so already because my mouth and chin were wet and sticky.

And I could hear voices; shouting, receding into the distance. No, just one voice. Someone I knew. Tigger.

Find Tigger. That's what I was here for. I tried to stand up but the world was made of mercury and it slip slided away before I could get a hold on it. And I had lost the torch but it didn't seem as dark as it had suddenly.

The mask. I was still wearing the stocking mask. That was why I couldn't see properly. I tried to peel it off but my hands came away wet and slippery. I ran them over the side of my face and it didn't seem to hurt but then it didn't seem to be my face either. Nothing felt familiar.

Then there was more light. I could see my feet and that was good because it meant I was upright and moving. And then there were figures coming at me out of the light. More monsters. And that I couldn't handle. I collapsed and hit my head and this time it really did hurt.

'Angel? Angel, are you all right?'

It was Mr Goodson, leaning over me so far that his pointed wizard's hat seemed almost at right-angles to his head.

'You took your time,' I said quite clearly.

'What? I can't understand what you're saying. Oh, good grief! What have they done to your teeth?'

The people of the local village were really rather cool about a black Austin taxi being driven through their midst by a guy in full wizard regalia. If they'd got a good look at me flopping about in the back like one of those nodding dogs with the strings cut, they would have called out the Neighbourhood Watch.

I had caught a glimpse of myself in the mirror as Mr Goodson had bundled me in and that had persuaded me not to try and take the stocking mask off. There was enough blood running down my throat already to convince me that something nasty had happened to the side of my face and I wasn't keen to have my suspicions confirmed.

'Where are you taking me?' I said, but it must have come out as something different.

'Don't worry,' said Mr Goodson, mishearing me. 'I can drive perfectly well. Once did the advanced drivers' challenge course in the Civil Service Motorists' Association.'

A man of many talents; most of them hidden. I decided not to argue with him and thought instead of the sun roof I had always meant to have had fitted into Armstrong. It would have been dead handy at the time as Mr Goodson's Grand Vizier's hat could have jutted out into space instead of having the top five inches bent out of shape. Of course, he could have taken it off, or I could have suggested that he did, but I was beginning to hurt and suddenly felt an overwhelming desire for drugs. Any drugs.

I usually keep a quarter bottle of vodka in the glove compartment for emergencies but I couldn't remember seeing it there earlier. I thought about asking Mr Goodson to check, but I knew he wouldn't approve of drinking and driving. Sod it, I wasn't driving.

'Can you reach into the glove compartment?' I asked quite succinctly. 'There should be some booze there, for medical purposes, of course.'

'It's getting on for six o'clock, but I wouldn't worry about that now.'

What was the man talking about? Didn't he understand plain English?

I gave up and slumped back in the seat. We were in a built-up area and I was awake enough to take in a passing sign saying HOSPITAL. Actually it just said 'H' but I'm fairly streetwise. I hoped the people in the hospital were because, dressed as we were and me in my condition, it could take some explaining. But as no one seemed to be able to understand a word I said, I decided to go with the flow.

As it turned out, the costumes saved us any difficult questions and got me seen pretty quickly. A bossy matron in Casualty (you ever seen a docile one?) wearing a face the colour of her uniform took one look at us as Mr Goodson half carried me in, and then exploded.

'Give me strength. It's that bloody Dungeons and Dragons place again. As if we didn't have enough normal people wanting medical attention for perfectly reasonable illnesses and complaints which were no fault of their own, we have to have these loonies paying good money to try and cripple each other. And it's not as if they're not old enough to know better.'

This last remark was aimed at Mr Goodson. Well, I was pretty sure it was but I wasn't going to argue. If I'd tried it would probably have come out as a telephone order for a Chinese take-away, so I kept quiet. Mr Goodson held his ground while holding me up, but quite wisely let the old bat run on until she had got her indignation out of her system and called the duty doctor to see me.

I remember lying down on a trolley and I remember a dark-haired, dark-eyed nurse (who later turned out to be called Mab, as in Queen of the Fairies, and who claimed she could do amazing things with a tube of lubricating jelly and a lot of imagination), but that was about it.

There was one other thing, an overheard conversation between Mr Goodson and whichever junior doctor was in the process of peeling off my stocking mask along with generous portions of skin.

The doctor was asking what sort of accident I'd had and Mr Goodson was being very diplomatic – you don't get to be a Grand Vizier for nothing – and bullshitting like fury. It was unheard of, he said. No it wasn't, said the young doctor, it was like Beirut on a busy day some Sundays in here. But all the weapons are harmless, Mr Goodson tried. They're all made of plastic or foam rubber.

He was right of course. But then again, the Armoury down in Nether World didn't get much call for woollen socks packed tight with coarse builder's sand and bits of broken brick.

I remember the nurse, Mab, was the one who took my clothes off and put me into a smock for the operating theatre.

I remember feeling hungry and complaining that they hadn't fed me, though no one could understand me. The matron snarled orders that I should be given a notebook and pencil if I was going to continue to cause trouble by remaining conscious. Fortunately she couldn't understand when I asked her what it had been like in the Waffen SS either.

I remember being wheeled down a corridor and into a lift and I remember somebody tagging my wrist with a clear plastic badge which just said 'Angel'. Now I didn't think that would inspire much confidence in the other patients, or visiting relatives, but nobody asked my opinion.

As I was about to be wheeled into surgery, another white coat (there had been about six by this time) leaned over me to look in my face, turning my chin in his hand and saying, 'Tch, tch, oh dear,' to himself.

Then he said: 'Well, we'll soon have you fixed up. We can do wonders these days.'

I signalled for the notebook and pencil and a male nurse offered them but matron grabbed his wrist and peered down at me.

'No more obscene drawings, eh, Mr Angel?'

I shook my head and mumbled, 'No.'

'Now, we promise, do we?' she asked icily.

'Absolutely,' I slurred, nodding as vigorously as I could.

She released the nurse's hand and I took the notebook. As I wrote I heard her say: 'I knew this one would be trouble,' to no one in particular.

I wrote: Will I be able to play the trumpet after the operation?

'Ignore him,' said matron. And when somebody asked why she said: 'It's the oldest one in the book. You tell him yes, of course he'll be able to play the trumpet after surgery. Then he writes back that that must be a miracle because he couldn't play going in. I've seen his type before. Anything for a cheap laugh.'

No, really. Wait.

Of course it looked much worse than it actually was. Everyone said so, so it must have been true, but they should have seen it from the inside.

There was a gash deep enough to have exposed the cheekbone, which is probably what Mr Goodson had seen. My teeth were all there, but some of them were smaller than they had been. Nothing about a thousand quid's worth of cosmetic dentistry couldn't put right, as one of the nurses quipped cheerily.

Talking was a problem for a couple of days as the whole of the right side of my face had ballooned out like a pregnant chipmunk on an eating binge. It was also blue. And black. And there were cute streaks of red in there too.

Because they were worried about a hairline fracture of something or other, the doctors made me wear a plastic protective shield which was supposed to be flesh-coloured except my flesh there wasn't pink any more. I just knew what people would say when they saw it.

To give him his due, Mr Goodson was the only one who did not state the grotesquely obvious when he visited me on the Sunday afternoon. Then again, he had been designated to visit by his fellow Grand Viziers to see if I was likely to sue them for what had happened.

I wrote copious notes assuring him that I wouldn't but I

made no attempt to elaborate on exactly what had happened. He was relieved by that and I was pretty sure Nether World would be. The hospital didn't think they had to ask me any more questions. And to be honest, they hadn't much liked the answers I had given them so far on the mundane stuff about diet or bedpans, so I doubted if they would call the cops or even think of doing so.

'I drove down in Armstrong,' Mr Goodson said nervously. 'I hope you don't mind. I filled up with diesel and I'm insured and everything.'

I mumbled that it was OK and wrote out a thank you for him driving me to the hospital.

'I didn't know whether to call the police or not,' he said. 'Not so much about you but about your friend.'

What friend? I wrote.

'I presumed it was. The one who seemed to be being pushed into that red Alfa Romeo. He didn't want to go and was shouting at the top of his voice. But then you came staggering out and . . .' His voice tailed off as he saw me scribbling on my notepad. He read the message.

'Yes I am sure it was a red Alfa. I've been a member of the Civil Service Motorists' Association for fifteen years. Why?'

I shook my head – gently – to indicate it was nothing. But it made sense of something at the back of my brain. When the Beast from the East had told me Bassotti was waiting for me in the McDonald's, he'd mentioned a red Alfa. Every time I had seen Bassotti, he'd been driving an old Sierra. My guess was that weasel-faced Sammy and his big friend had been waiting for me to lead them to Nether World and Tigger. I had been set up to set up Tigger.

'Are you sure there's nothing I can do for you?' Mr Goodson asked.

How do you feel about giving somebody a driving lesson or two?

Duncan and his wife Doreen were my next visitors and they took one look at the plastic face mask and said together: 'It's the Phantom of the Opera.' I counted that as two.

Duncan came again on the Monday, bringing Bunny with him.

I hadn't seen Bunny since we'd done the Marengi gig together in the club off Oxford Street. He said that he had only come to offer me some more playing dates, but in fact Bunny would go anywhere there were nurses. 'They all wear black stockings and suspenders,' he told me enthusiastically.

No they don't, I wrote. None of them. Trust me on this one.

He took it badly.

Doogie and Miranda turned up once, made the obligatory Phantom observation (twenty-six by this time) and ate the fruit they had brought.

Why was it always fruit for hospital visits? If you're in hospital you need a stiff drink or a smoke, not fruit. There are people there paid to keep you healthy; amateurs shouldn't meddle.

I had cards from people I didn't know knew my address let alone which hospital I was in. And I had cards from people I know I had deliberately not told my address. I had phone messages from a 'Mr Springsteen' saying that he was eating well, which I guessed was Fenella, and one from Nassim, our beloved landlord, saying this week's rent could wait given the special circumstances. Big of him.

I could more or less articulate again, in fact I was demanding a discharge on the basis that 'Surely you need the bed', when I had a visit from Crimson. It was not that I wasn't pleased to see him, just surprised.

'I was on a job in the area,' he said to prove it was no big deal. 'Just thought I'd drop in. My God, man, you look like –'

One hundred and thirty-four.

'Cut the sweet-talk, what're you after?'

'Hey, man, can't I do the full hospital visit for a friend? I thought you were supposed to sit by the bed and look at your watch every five minutes. I had it all planned.'

'Did you bring any booze?'

'Nope.'

'Any drugs?'

'What? *Into* a hospital? You concussed, man?'

'Any grapes?'

'Huh?'

'Bananas, pineapples, kiwi fruit, those ugly little horned melons you get down the supermarket that nobody knows what to do with?'

'No, man, no fruit.'

'Then you are naff-all use as a hospital visitor. I'm out of here tomorrow or next day, tops. Don't prolong the agony.'

He smiled nervously and reached inside his leather biker's jacket.

'I brought you a newspaper, man.'

Suddenly, he wasn't kidding around.

It was the *Evening Standard* from the day before, an early afternoon edition, not that that mattered. Crimson had opened it at page five and he pointed to the column of news-in-brief stories just in case I missed the point.

An inquest had opened (and adjourned immediately pending further investigation) on one Christopher Robin O'Neil, whose naked body had been found butting up against Blackfriars Bridge on an incoming tide on Saturday night. That was the gist of it although there was a 'See page 14' tag line.

Page fourteen was a feature article about the perils of London's homeless drug abusers, written by a minor academic who found that broad brush-stroke analysis paid better than actual research. The article gave the impression that all London's homeless were (a) drug crazed, and (b) simply queuing up to take their clothes off and jump in the Thames.

I read as much as I could stomach, which wasn't much. The key bit was in the intro where it said that 'in a week when' the body of a sixteen-year-old boy could be fished from the river and be identified because he was a registered drug abuser and had a police record, wasn't it about time somebody did something? Well, hell yes, it probably was.

I looked at Crimson and he met my stare.

'So this guy is Tigger? Is that what you're saying?'

'Can't be two, man,' said Crimson. 'And I figured what with you asking around after him, and you being the bloodest of blood brothers, you might know what happened to him.'

'I don't know,' I said honestly. 'But I think I know a man who does.'

13

'Miss Binkworthy really has come on in leaps and bounds over the last few days,' said Mr Goodson.

'Only because Mr Goodson is such a patient teacher,' said Fenella smugly.

'Pass the sick bag,' I said from the back seat of the dual-control Metro, but they didn't hear me.

When I had seen Fenella with Mr Goodson as they arrived to collect me on my discharge, I had automatically assumed that he had brought Armstrong back and I was to be driven home in style, with Fenella cradling my head to her bosom while I sipped vodka and orange through a straw. Not only had they forgotten the vodka, but Fenella had pleaded illness and left her office early in order to squeeze in an extra driving lesson. Never mind my state of health and the need to avoid nasty shocks or nervous stress. I just had to sit there, eyes closed, and suffer. Dead selfish, some people.

I made them stop once on the pretext that I had a prescription for some painkillers and needed a pharmacy. The fact that there was an off-licence next door was purely coincidental. While Fenella tried, without notable success, to park the Metro roughly parallel to the kerb, I staggered into the pharmacy to start negotiations over the prescription. As I had guessed, the pills prescribed by the doctor who discharged me were simply double-strength versions of a commercial brand which cost one-fifth the price of the prescription. I bought a hundred of the proprietary brand and tore the prescription up, even though I knew I could have made a few quid on it in certain circles. I also bought a packet of children's bendy straws which helped me drink the can of Special Brew I picked up at the off-licence. Double the dose of pills

143

and a few slurps of lager and I was far better equipped to cope with the journey back to Hackney. Keeping my eyes closed helped too.

To be fair, we made it back without incident, unless you count the close encounter with a bus near Blackfriars Bridge, but as Fenella didn't even see it, I didn't count it.

At Stuart Street, they hadn't exactly put out flags to mark my return, but somebody had cleaned up the flat and bought in a pint of milk and half a dozen cans of soup, all approved by the Vegetarian Society. Not a smoke or a decent drink in the place. And no sign of Springsteen, though that was a relief. He would only have howled at me. Not because there was anything wrong as such, he just liked howling at me and had five days of moaning stored up. And he would have laughed at the flesh-coloured plastic cheek mask I had been advised to wear for another week.

The mask still made it difficult for me to talk; or, rather, I could talk perfectly well but people somehow didn't hear me properly.

'I've got something for you,' Fenella said from the kitchen where she was battling with the can opener. 'It's in there, in the cupboard.'

I was in the bathroom, easing off my face mask and, in the cupboard mirror, checking all the places I'd missed while trying to shave over the last few days.

I grunted something to her and opened the cupboard door to find a plastic jar which rattled with pills and which had a handwritten label saying 'Arnica'. There was a leaflet with the jar printed by a company called Pain Relief From Plants Ltd and which told me all about the healing properties of arnica, a natural plant extract. I touched my cheek and jaw and felt like ordering a fieldful. The leaflet said it was ideal for the reduction of bruising and had no harmful side effects or hallucinogenic qualities. What a waste of time.

'Soup's on,' yelled Fenella, 'and I've put some more stuff down for Springsteen.'

'Meat,' I mumbled, 'it's called meat.'

'No, I can't stop to eat, anyway, there's only enough for

144

one. Mr Goodson is doing three-point turns with me tonight, so I've got to get ready. See you.'

Now if ever anything needed a smart-mouth answer, that did, but although I thought it, my mouth let me down. It also almost refused to accept the three bean and chive soup she had left for me but somehow I slurped some down, knowing I would need all my strength to do the really difficult things I had to do, like use the phone.

As it turned out, it was a brief call.

'H.B. Builders. Please leave a message after the tones.'

I probably shouldn't have driven after all the painkillers I had chewed that afternoon, but there are lots of things I probably shouldn't do. (Rule of Life No. 11: A 'probably shouldn't' has approximately half the risk factor of a 'Why did I?' and thirty per cent of that of a 'Why the hell not?')

It didn't take me long to get over to Stratford Marsh, despite the rush hour traffic, though there was one sticky moment when two young lads in a Thames van advertising their window-cleaning business pulled up alongside Armstrong at some lights. Even above the sound of Armstrong's diesel and their idling engine and the Bryan Ferry tape played at full whack, I could lip-read one saying to the other that I looked just like the Phantom of the Opera. Two hundred and three.

I turned into the Navigation Road Industrial Estate and did a drive-by of H.B. Builders to scout the lie of the land. The gates were closed and there was no sign of life. Not unusual. It was a little after six p.m. and few builders' yards stayed open that late. What was unusual was that a big CLOSED sign had been hung on the padlock and chain which bound the gates together.

I turned Armstrong round and did a run back, slowing down to scope the place properly. Nothing. No sign of life, no lights, no vehicles.

The only place open at all in the area seemed to be a greasy spoon (greasy fork, greasy knife) café round the corner. That had a sign in the window saying 'Breakfasts All Day'. It sounded like a threat.

I parked Armstrong and after checking in the mirror, decided to remove my cheek mask. People might gasp at the multi-coloured bruise, though it was fading, but at least that might get me some sympathy instead of Lon Chaney jokes.

The café was just called 'Café', which was just as well as even that probably contravened the Trade Descriptions Act. It was certainly the freshest thing about the place. The tables only matched in the sense that they were all made of wood and plastic to some degree or other. They all had salt cellars and sugar bowls and ketchup but no two containers or brands matched. Even the menu chalked on a wall-mounted blackboard had been written in a variety of coloured chalks, although obviously by the same person as the spelling was consistently bad. Actually, thinking about the overall chaotic effect, if they could have moved the place up to the West End, or maybe Chelsea Harbour, and served something other than chips, then they could have tripled their prices and made a fortune.

The tall, lanky youth behind the counter glared at me from under the shank of black hair he had trained to fall over his right eye. He wiped the counter with a dirty grey cloth as I drew near. The body language was clear. Don't try asking for a full breakfast at this time of night. Mate.

'Just a coffee, please,' I said and the words came out roughly right, at least he seemed to understand me. Maybe people talked like that around here.

'Cappuccino, espresso or ordinary?' he asked, spoiling me for choice.

'The frothy one,' I said, not convinced I could manage 'cappuccino' and anyway, it was the least suspicious one to have to drink with a spoon.

It was surprisingly good cappuccino and seemed to be a popular item judging by the rings of foam which had dried on the outside of the cup. The lad behind the counter watched me through his curtain of hair, waiting for a complaint. There was no one else in the place to complain so I felt sorry to have to disappoint him.

I was wondering how to engage him in conversation short of picking a fight with him, when I spotted the notice board next to the blackboard menu. It was just a pin board with numerous visiting cards drawing-pinned there offering a variety of services, though not those you find advertised in telephone boxes. There were minicabs and 24-hour plumbers, as you might have expected. There were also a couple of surprising ones, like 'Shiatsu Massage in Your Home' (I hear in the street, it's still an offence) to an advert for the Convention on Cryptozoology (Barking Branch) offering lectures on 'Unknown Hominids'. The New Age had even reached Stratford. Was nowhere safe?

I stood up and pointed to the one printed on pink card which advertised H.B. Builders.

'Is that the firm just down the road?' I tried and the youth understood me perfectly.

'Well it was, mate, until they turned up their toes this week,' he said chattily. 'Last Friday, they was there working full belt. First thing Monday morning, shop shut, gone away, staff all get given the DCM medal.'

The DCM – Don't Come Monday – redundancy.

'That was a bit sudden, wasn't it? I was round there last week asking for a price on a job.'

'Too bloody right it was. Dead previous as me mum would say. 'Course, it's hit our trade as well. This place used to be a gold mine.'

If he meant by that dirty and ill-lit, you had to agree with him.

'So what's the score? Somebody do a runner?'

'Looks like the boss did.' Then, over his shoulder he yelled: 'Doesn't it, Kelly?'

The swing door behind him opened and the girl I'd last seen in Bassotti's office stood there, drying her hands on a grease-streaked apron. The Doc Martens' were the same, but the punk make-up had gone, replaced by a harassed, washed-out look which would never catch on.

'Doesn't it what?' she asked, giving me the eye. I could see recognition dawning slowly.

'Your old boss, Bertie. Looks like he's done a runner, eh?'

'Well, I was ready to give him the benefit of the doubt, yer know,' Kelly started generously.

'Until Tuesday,' said the youth.

'Well, yer know, it's just that, like, he hasn't even tried to get in touch. I mean, yer know, we all turn up for work on Monday, well some of us do, yer know, and it's like a ghost town. All locked up – padlock on the gate even. No sign of Bert – Mr Bassotti – *and* he owes me two days' overtime.'

'Well, you can kiss that,' said the youth, though nobody had asked him.

'Nobody asked you, Clint,' said Kelly, reading my mind. Then she conceded: 'But he's probably right, yer know.'

'And no sign of Mr Bassotti since?' I asked, trying to get the most out of them before they wondered why I was asking in the first place.

'Not a sniff. I hung around for hours on Monday but I couldn't even get in the office. A couple of the casuals turned up but didn't hang around long. So, yer know, I came round here to see Clint and use the phone.'

'And walked straight into another job,' smirked Clint. 'Not bad, eh, these days?'

'Job?' snorted Kelly. 'Bleedin' slave labour's more like it. But beggars can't be choosers and Bassotti doesn't look like he'll be making up the wages this week.'

'Did you ring him at home?' I tried, riding my luck.

''Course I did, but there was no bleedin' answer, was there? Haven't got through all week.'

'That's his house in – Dagenham, isn't it?' I guessed.

'Naw, he lives in Romford, always has.' She looked at me curiously, trying to work out if she'd been conned in some way or other. (Rule of Life No. 83: Approached in the right way, anyone will tell you anything and it will usually be true.)

'But he's not answering the phone, eh?' I asked, filing away the idea that there couldn't be that many Bassottis with first initial 'U' in the Romford phone book. (And if he'd been ex-directory, let's face it, he wouldn't have given his number to motormouth Kelly.)

'Is there an echo in here?' she said sarcastically. 'I said I've tried every day, didn't I? So anyway, yesterday I blew him out and left an earbashing on his answerphone at work.'

'And a right earbash it was too, I can tell you,' Clint added. 'Some serious GBH of the lugholes there, mate.'

'He loves that answerphone,' Kelly smiled. 'I used to call it his Godbox.'

'I have to ask,' I said, trying to smile, but in my state it must have come out like a leer. 'Why Godbox?'

''Cos he got his orders from above on it. Every time there was a message he'd kick me out so he could listen to it in private. Maybe he had a bit on the side, I don't know, but listening to his messages was one of the highlights of his day.'

'He probably had some tart make obscene calls so he could pull his own chain,' Clint volunteered. 'You know, cream his own jeans.'

'Don't be gross,' Kelly admonished, smirking as she did so.

'What sort of an answerphone was it?' I tried innocently, but my credit limit had just been reached.

'How should I know? It was a black one, with long-play tapes. He bought it from Abdul's Electrics round the corner. Said it was the only thing he'd ever bought there that worked.'

'How come you're so interested anyway?' Clint said in his most macho voice. Even in my wrecked and weakened state, I wasn't too worried about him. Kelly, on the other hand, scared the hell out of me.

'Yeah,' she said, wising up, 'how come you're so interested in Bert?'

'You saw me there last week,' I said as if that explained everything.

'Well, yeah . . .'

'You were wearing those red hot pants and you can't expect me to have forgotten those.'

'Yeah, that's right.' She blushed. She actually blushed and Clint glared at her.

'And if it's any consolation, you're not the only one the bugger owes wages to.'

'Well, if you find him first, don't forget me will you?' she said coyly, or what for her passed for coy.

'How could I?' I said honestly.

*

I had assumed that 'Abdul's Electrics' was local lazy slang to cover any East End trader not obviously white or called Harry, in much the same way that people refer to late-opening shops as 'Patels' these days. The Patels ought to get organized and register a trade name.

As it turned out, the shop down the road was actually called Abdul's Electrics but was in fact run by a depressive Scot who wore a badge saying 'You can call me Jock' and who had bought the business from Abdul the year before. I knew all this because he had a hand-written sign stuck to the cash register explaining it all. I guessed instantly that here was a man who could turn ugly if he heard one more Abdul reference.

Yes, he did do a black answerphone, just the one, and his tone suggested that he didn't believe for a minute I was in the market for it. Still, he went through the motions, looking at his watch to let me know I was keeping him. But then again, where does it say you have to be civil?

Naturally the one I wanted was right at the back of the top shelf. That produced a few under-the-breath curses and while he was reaching for it, I checked my profile in the video monitor he had set up as a demo model. The bruising on my cheek was still vivid but no longer glowing in the dark. I looked up to see Jock watching me watching myself on the monitor, so I smiled at him. It did look like a leer. I must watch that.

The answerphone was a Telecom model with push buttons, a limited memory and remote function for dialling, all the standard jazz. I lifted it out of its box and tried to look interested.

Underneath the machine itself, nestling in the styrofoam packaging, was the instruction book and all the other bits and pieces they give you: the guarantee card, little bits of sticky paper to write your number on, screws and raw plugs for mounting the thing on the wall. There was also the one thing I wanted and when I said to Jock that I'd like to see a white one before I completed my market research, he turned with a sigh to reach for another box, and I palmed it. I wasn't even worried about the camcorder filming us, I was confident the palm went smoothly.

I made all the noises Jock was waiting to hear about how I'd think about it and get back to him and I left him packing the phones back into their boxes.

He never noticed that one of them was now missing its handy, wallet-size plastic-coated card which told you how to ring in from a remote phone and collect the messages on your new, black Telecom answerphone.

I wasn't going to waste much time in Romford because Armstrong was the wrong sort of vehicle for a long surveillance job. In the middle of town no one notices a black cab, not even one parked for a suspiciously long period in the same place. But out in commuter land where the houses have gaps between them, taxis mean someone is coming and going. Taxis parked and not moving draw attention.

So I found a garage and filled up with diesel (apparently something beyond the powers of a Grand Vizier) and looked up Bassotti in the local phone book. I had been right; there was only one with the initial 'U' and he lived on Peveral Road. The garageman behind his armoured screen took great delight in giving what appeared to be a London cabbie street directions, and I took it with suitable humility.

Out of sight of the garage I found a phone box and tried the number listed for the Peveral Road address. No answer; and no answerphone.

Peveral Road was semi-detached country with front gardens down to the road. I found Number 27 easily enough, it was the one house on the street in total darkness, and parked outside under a streetlight. Nothing suspicious in that. Any inquisitive neighbour could see that a black London cab had pulled up and there was a London cabbie going about his lawful business, walking up the garden path to ring the front doorbell.

And when there was no answer, what more natural than for the aforementioned cabbie to start knocking loudly, then pacing around the bay window, trying to look in. And then, his normally limitless patience fast expiring, he goes next door, where the net curtains have been twitching all along and rings the bell there.

So that really is 27 Peveral Road, party name of Bassotti? Ordered a computer cab an hour ago for a trip up West? What? Nobody there since Monday? Well, bugger me if people don't take liberties, eh? And I'd come all the way from Great Portland Street for this? And naturally I'm sorry to disturb you, 'cos you're not the sort to call cabs out on wild goose chases, but are you sure nobody's been there since Monday? Oh, did an early morning flit did they? Really? Suitcases and all? In a minicab? There, that proves it. Can you trust people who use minicabs instead of proper, licensed hackney carriages? Of course you can't. Bet the bloke was running out on his missus. Oh, so the wife was with him, was she? And the kids? And this was early Monday morning? Five a.m., eh, as early as that? And not a word except a note to the milkman? Some people, eh?

Some people.

I had Bassotti's number at H.B. Builders from the business card he had given me, and I had the card which told me how to do a remote interrogation on his answerphone. Unless, of course, he had been clever enough to add in a security code to stop people like me doing what I was going to do. The trouble with programming in a code, though, was that you could only use it yourself via a touch tone keypad phone (the ones which play tunes when you dial). Unless you could always guarantee access to one, you were limited to how and when you could pick up your messages, so most people never bothered adding the security back-up.

Back home at Stuart Street, I made myself as comfortable as possible with the house phone tucked under my left cheek. I don't think I could have fitted it under my right. Then I dialled H.B. Builders and got the answerphone message telling me to speak after the tones.

From then on I followed the instructions on the Telecom card.

After the beep, keep quiet for six seconds until a single beep.

Then speak for five seconds without pause ('So there was this bloke called Harry who went into work one day and said no, this morning it's Lucky Harry and the doorman says why? And Harry answers . . .') until you hear two more beeps.

Then remain silent for four seconds until you hear three beeps.

Then speak for four seconds ('. . . I was running for the bus and I saw a ladder up against a wall and I said I'm not going under that and the first person who did got a pot of paint right on the head so I said it's lucky . . .') until a single beep.

If there are no messages, the machine beeps rapidly. If there are, it rewinds the tape and plays them to you. Down the line, the tape whirred.

'Bert? Listen, it's Hubbard. There was no need for you to go tearing off like that last night. You knew the little prick had it coming to him. Anyway, he won't try and shaft us again. Sammy had some stuff that kept him quiet and you won't hear any more about it. Trust me. Just keep your cool, OK? I'll call you next week and get some more drops sorted.'

Click.

The next message was from a punter in Stepney who wasn't convinced the dampcourse H.B. Builders had put in was working and he wanted his money back. The other three were from Kelly, starting out rude and ending obscene.

It had been first time lucky for me, if not for Tigger.

14

Stop. Rewind. Pause. Frame advance.

My jaw and teeth were beginning to throb, so I took four co-proxamol painkillers and an anti-inflammatory pill at one go. The instructions on the box said do not mix with alcohol but I had rescued the emergency vodka from Armstrong to help wash them down just to make sure they did their job. Within five minutes, I couldn't feel my face. My kinda painkillers.

I knew I had about ten minutes more before the old eyelids snapped shut like a barmaid's smile at closing time, so I lay on my bed and tried to think it through.

I had Tigger connected to Bassotti and Bassotti connected to someone called Hubbard, presumably the Hubbard of Hubbard's scrap yard where Tigger had insisted we dump the last loads of whatever it was we were being paid to dump. I also had another link, though I hadn't let on to anyone, and that was the weasel-faced individual I had recognized as one of the two who jumped Tigger and put me in need of cosmetic dentistry. Presumably the same 'Sammy' referred to on the tape.

Then there was what Tigger had said; something about Lee. He hadn't told Lee anything because he knew he had a loose mouth. Told him about what? Not where he was, because Lee knew he went 'monstering'; it was just that in his chemically challenged state he wasn't sure what that meant. No, I reasoned with myself, there was something else Tigger hadn't told Lee, but whether that was because he did not trust him or because he wanted to protect him, I couldn't know.

And if I wanted to find out, I had three options. The first

was to ask Bassotti, which wasn't on as he'd done a runner. The second was to go see this Hubbard guy and risk ending up trying to drink the Thames dry like Tigger had. The third was to talk to Lee, but I didn't know where he was. Still, I'd found him once before, hadn't I? Where was the problem?

The problem was that someone had hung weights from my eyelids and had wired up an amplifier to my lungs so that each breath seemed to boom around my head. I went under and dreamt of nothing worth remembering.

I awoke after ten hours' solid. It would have been longer had not Springsteen been pacing up and down the bed plucking at the duvet with his claws looking for an opening so he could get at bare flesh.

'OK, OK, I'm up. Breakfast is served,' I muttered, more to give my jaw exercise than to make conversation with him. He's such a grump in the mornings. 'Who needs an alarm clock with you around?'

I was in the kitchen halfway through pulling the ring-pull on a can of cat food (a great innovation and once they make them paw and claw friendly, will negate the need for humans almost entirely) when I thought: Lee does.

When I had found Lee in Lincoln's Inn, he'd had an alarm clock inside his sleeping bag. I doubted if he had to get up to catch a train to the office each morning, and it had looked new come to think of it. What did Lee have to get up for?

Springsteen circled my feet and howled impatiently.

Doc. It must be Doc. Tigger had said she did an early morning round in Lincoln's Inn. Maybe Lee was on her list of regular patients now. God knows he ought to be somebody's.

Springsteen took a lump out of my calf and this time it was me howling.

I checked Lincoln's Inn just in case, but it was after eleven a.m. when I got there and there was no sign of life. Sure, there were a few tents there and the more permanent bashas but there was no sign of Lee or his new dome tent. There were signs of a more ominous nature in that a wire fence had been erected around the perimeter of the Fields, allowing access only to the gates. At intervals around the fence were printed notices in small, official print. I didn't need to get close enough to read them to know what they would say. The Empire was striking back. It was hit the road time for the residents of Cardboard City.

I cruised the Gray's Inn Road until I was fairly sure I recognized the house where Doc and Tigger had taken Lee to fix his smashed-up hand. The bell push didn't help. It just listed the flats, six of them, with no names. The occupants valued their privacy. I could handle that.

I pressed all six buzzers with the flat of my hand and kept it there.

'What the fuck . . . hey? Who's that?' was the first response from a distorted, tinny but undoubtedly male voice.

It was impossible to tell which flat it had come from, but at least it was a response.

'I'm looking for the Doc, man,' I said dreamily.

'We're all fucking doctors here,' he snapped back. 'And some of us have been on night shift.'

'Hey, sorry, man,' I said, resisting the temptation to tell him to try tranquillizers. 'I'm after the Doc, the lady doc. The one from the Fields, man.'

'Oh shit, you want Sandy. Flat 2.'

'Thanks, man. You ought to get more sleep, you know. Working nights takes it out of you.'

But he'd gone.

I pressed the button for Flat 2 and heard a voice asking: 'Yeah? Whaddayawant?'

I leaned into the doorbell unit and said: 'Doc? Is that Doc from Lincoln's Inn?'

'Could be. Who's that?'

'I'm a friend of Tigger's. We brought a kid here a coupla weeks ago. Kid with a smashed hand. You fixed him up.'

'Can't say I know what you're talking about,' she said chattily. 'And what's it to you anyway?'

I could detect a transatlantic twang in her voice which was coming over the intercom as clear as a bell.

'Listen,' I pleaded, 'I don't really want to talk about this out here. Can I come in?' No response. 'Look, Tigger's in trouble.'

'Yeah. We have a medical term for the kind of trouble Tigger's in.'

'Really? What's that?' I had to ask.

'Dead. It's quite common really and nothing to be ashamed of.'

I did a double-take at the bell box, not quite believing I was having this conversation. She took pity on me.

'Look up,' she said and I did and there she was leaning out of a second-floor window looking down on me.

'OK, you can come up.' She nodded her head towards where Armstrong was parked. 'I recognized the cab.'

She disappeared inside and the door buzzed off its lock and I tramped in and climbed the stairs to where she had the door to her flat already open.

She was wearing a long T-shirt which came down to her knees. The front of it was entirely given over to a reprint of the cover of an old, green Penguin paperback: Raymond Chandler's *The Long Goodbye*. The penguin logo fell diplomatically just around her crotch.

'What are you looking at?' she said, leaning back against a table, arms out to the side, giving me a good view.

'I enjoy a good read,' I said truthfully.

'I have another one which reads: "Go Beat Your Meat, I'm Married".'

'Have you? Are you?'

'No, not really. Now what do you want? And what have you done to your face?'

At last. Either the medic or the mother in her was coming out. She came over to me and gently touched my cheek and she was close enough for me to tell that the T-shirt was all she was wearing. I was going to miss the bruising when it went, in an odd sort of way.

'I got hit with a sockful of sand,' I said, knowing she would have heard worse.

'Don't give me that. You fell downstairs or walked into a door. That's what they usually say. Does it hurt?'

She touched me slightly, probably not hard enough to

crease a cigarette paper, but I yelped and jumped backwards.

'So it does. You ought to be wearing one of those plastic cheek guards, if you can stand all the morons saying you look like the Phantom of the Opera.'

'They wouldn't, would they?'

'And I hope you know a friendly dentist. You'll not get that lot rebuilt on the National Health, or if you do you'll have to wait so long you might as well put in for the dentures now.'

'What do you tell your patients who are really ill, doctor?' I tried my most winning smile but could feel it coming out at an angle.

'I don't have any. I'm not a doctor, yet. Just a student.'

'You seem to have a thriving practice out in Lincoln's Inn.'

'Most of those injuries are self-inflicted and anyway, they're the sort of patient who would run a mile rather than check into a hospital.'

'I've asked around,' I lied. 'You do good work.'

'Somebody has to.'

She moved away from me, over to a Habitat sofa – the sort that converts into a bed if you don't mind eyeballing the mice while you lie there – and sat down, curling her legs under her. She nodded to the armchair and I sat down after a quick scope of the room. Medical textbooks, a jar of coffee and a kettle, a midi CD system and a set of headphones. The girl travelled light.

'Was Tigger one of your patients?' I opened.

'I don't have patients yet. Call him a customer.' She flicked hair back from her face although she hadn't needed to. 'A very good customer. And he brought me lots of others.'

'Like Lee.'

'I don't know their names. Not while they're still breathing, anyway.'

'So how did you hear of Tigger's death?'

'I heard. The cops run checks. They know about people like me, like us, in this house. Shit, one or two have even brought kids here before now. Nowhere else to go. Some of them on the street call us that, you know. Nowhere. They say they're going to Nowhere because there's nowhere else to go. That's us, Nowhere Patrol.'

'Like you said, someone's gotta do it.'

'Shouldn't have to. What's your stake in all this? How did you hear about Tigger?'

'Newspaper. I'd been looking for him, but somebody else found him first.'

I waited to see how that went down. She could have thrown me out then. Maybe I would have thanked her if she had.

Instead she narrowed her eyes and said: 'Your name's Angel, isn't it?'

'I thought you said no names.'

'You're not a customer, are you?'

'No.' There but for the grace of whatever, though.

'That's cool then. Do you know how he died?'

'Fished out of the river, I read. Don't know the details.'

'I do. I asked around.' She caught my look. 'Fellow medics, a friendly cop. Professional interest, that's all.'

'And?'

'Tigger was streetwise. He knew most of the heroin in this town is no more than thirty-five per cent pure. That's the way it's cut to insure maximum economies of scale, give a satisfying kick and not damage the end-user too much too soon, so they develop a habit which is manageable as long as they have the cash.

'Now Tigger may have dabbled with drugs of all sorts. OK, let's get real, the guy was a walking cocktail cabinet at times, but he wasn't mainlining. So why did he shoot himself up with stuff that the forensic boys estimate was over eighty per cent pure?'

'Good question,' I said limply. I was getting an awful feeling that my bruised jaw and smashed teeth meant I had got off lightly.

'*Fucking* good question, actually, and like all the best questions, is one that isn't getting asked. Tigger was known as a user, however infrequent. He came into possession of some outstanding shit and used it. Whoops, there goes another

159

one. If the needle hadn't got him, then the HIV would have. Case closed.'

She flicked the nails of her right thumb and index finger to make a rapid clicking noise. I wondered how long she'd quit smoking.

'Why are you telling me all this? Isn't this some kind of privileged information?'

'Who hit you with the sockful of sand?' She made eye contact and hung in there.

'Now that *is* classified.'

'Same person who wanted to fly Tigger to the moon?'

'Could be.'

'Then I'll tell you anything that will help you nail them.'

'Whoa, hold on.' I was halfway out of my seat. 'What makes you think I'm out to nail anyone?'

'A, because you're asking, and b, because somebody has to. I'll help.'

'Then tell me where Lee is.'

'Don't know who you're talking about.'

'The young kid Tigger and I brought here in Arm . . . in my cab. Had a smashed-up hand and was wired on Amp.'

'Doesn't mean a thing.' She stared me out until I got it.

'OK, I see. Supposing Tigger had a friend who may or may not be called Lee, who may or may not have come here at some point in the past. I last saw him in Lincoln's Inn Fields last week. Do you think, hypothetically, that such a person might still be there?'

'Hypothetically, I think there's a chance you might find such a person there tonight.'

'And if not, then tomorrow morning around seven-thirty a.m.?'

'How did you know that?'

'Lee has an alarm clock. Who else would he get up for in the morning?'

She allowed her mouth to curve. 'He doesn't always see me as an angel of mercy.'

'I'll bet. Some guys don't know when they have it made. What's he on?'

'Physeptone, it's an injectable drug replacement.'

'I know.'

'But not strictly on prescription, so to speak.'

'I hear it's harder to get off than the H it's replacing.'

'It's been said. It helps if you don't experiment with everything else on the periodic table while you're trying to cold turkey.'

'Life sucks sometimes,' I said, to lighten the mood.

'No, life's OK,' said Doc slowly. 'It's just people who screw it up.'

There was nothing much to say to that.

'You know something, Angel? We have one basic rule here on the Nowhere Patrol: no names. Few questions, no names, no records, no files, no blacklists. Somebody's been doing Nowhere Patrol for over twenty-five years now and there's not one piece of paper to prove it. Guys who were junior interns in the Sixties did this and now they're called "Mr" and charge five hundred bucks an hour in Harley Street. The surgeons do their cutting before three p.m. in the summer, eleven a.m. in the winter. That's so they can make the golf course with daylight to spare.'

I wondered where this was going but I wasn't going to interrupt.

'Doctors, real doctors, who did the Nowhere Patrol ten years ago now think of kids on the street as just an obstruction to them finding a parking slot for their BMWs. People forget. They forget that twenty years ago they were sneaking condoms to girls too young or too spaced out to go on the pill, and that was when we thought the pill was safe. Today we plead with the rent boys to carry condoms. Always. Even when you're least likely to score; say, for example, if you were to hang out in the amusement arcade near Cambridge Circus every afternoon hoping to trap some elderly perv on a cheap-day return ticket from the provinces.'

'Would that be the one on Charing Cross Road? Hypothetically, of course.'

'Perhaps,' she said, relaxing, leaning her head back as if to get a better look at me.

'Doc, you are a very good person.'

'No, I'm not.' She blinked twice. 'Stick around and I'll show you.'

I looked at my watch.

'I thought I had a date up near Cambridge Circus,' I said.

She stood up and walked over to me, reaching out to air-brush my cheek with her fingertips.

'I said late afternoon, didn't I? I meant late afternoon. Hypothetically, that is.'

'Look,' I tried, but not too hard, 'I know the doctor usually knows best, but I've kinda been in the wars lately.'

'Don't worry,' she said, so close now I could hear her heart. 'I won't go anywhere near your face.'

Even though I was looking for him, Lee wasn't easy to spot; not at first, anyway. He was just one of maybe a dozen kids playing the pinball machines and the electronic 'Terminator' shooting ranges or Grand Prix driving skills games. (I filed away the idea of a perfect Christmas present for Fenella when I saw those.)

They were all dressed the same way. Trainers, jogging pants or shell suit bottoms and some sort of brightly coloured rainproof top, though a couple wore satin-effect jackets emblazoned with the names and logos of American football teams. The Raiders were in, it seemed, because they'd read somewhere that the Los Angeles gangs favoured them. At least it proved they could read something other than a video scoreboard.

Lee was hogging the 'Jurassic Park' pinball machine. When those had first arrived there had been queues. He was rocking back on the heels of a pair of hi-tops, connected to the machine only by the tips of his middle fingers on the buttons. His score was passable, but might have been better if he'd had his eyes open.

'Hello there, Lee.'

He swayed some more and said, 'Hi' in a dreamy sort of voice. Then he stopped rocking on his heels and opened his eyes, trying to focus on me in the reflection from the machine.

'D'I know you?'

I wondered just how spaced he was, or whether it was all just part of his sales pitch.

'We've met. Twice, actually. I'm a friend of Tigger's and we need to talk.'

I had spoken quietly and there was enough background noise in the arcade to cover anything short of a personal rape alarm going off. It was modern-day background musak, the constant beep-beep whirring of electronic bleeps punctuated by synthesized vocal effects like 'Go, dude' and 'A for excellent, hombre'. Lee just stood there as if taking it all in, his fingers frozen on the flipper buttons.

The last silver ball in his game rolled safely by the claws of a Tyrannosaurus Rex and headed straight for the gap between the two flippers. Lee made no attempt to stop it.

'Game over,' I said, about two seconds before the machine did. The effect was more dramatic than I would have thought possible.

'I've wet myself,' said Lee softly and then he started to cry.

I put an arm on his shoulder.

'Come on, there's a pub round the corner where we can talk.'

He was eighty thousand points short of a reply, in more ways than one. His fingers seemed welded to the machine. This was ridiculous. He was resisting the pressure of my arm by anchoring himself with the tips of two fingers. I said 'Come on' again and used my left hand in the small of his back to steer him clear of the machine. Another kid about the same age was inserting money in it before Lee's fingerprints were cold.

He took a couple of steps, stiff-legged. His chin was down on his chest which heaved as he gulped back the tears.

Out of the corner of my eye I caught sight of the arcade manager, or one of his heavies, getting up from his seat in the change booth. I turned my blue-and-black cheek towards him and held up my right hand, palm up, mouthing the words 'No problem' and shaking my head.

He sat down again. He'd seen worse things.

Out on the pavement I gave Lee the once over. If he tugged his jacket down at the front, no one would notice, I told him.

I gave him a couple of only slightly used Kleenex and steered him by the elbow round the corner and into the Spice of Life.

Though it is far from the most famous pub in Soho, the Spice is probably the most aptly named with, as they used to say, all human life being there. Fortunately, it being late afternoon, only a cross-section of all human life was in, so we were able to get a table near the door.

'There's a pub rule,' I told Lee. 'The landlord's Irish and he insists on everyone enjoying themselves. So stop crying or we'll get chucked out.'

Lee sniffed loudly and looked around.

'I want to go to the toilet,' he said.

The door marked GENTLEMEN was about two feet away.

'Through there and down the stairs,' I said. 'I won't come with you. That's a chucking-out offence here as well.'

'Get me a double orange juice, would you?' he asked as he headed for the toilets, clutching his crutch. I hoped the barman hadn't seen him.

I turned to see the barman and the three customers at the bar all staring at me. I moved towards them rapidly, figuring that using the toilet before spending any money there was also grounds for being asked to leave.

'A pint of your excellent McMullen's IPA, please,' I smarmed.

'Is he eighteen?' the barman came back snappily. Another dismissal offence.

'And a large orange juice, please.'

The barman nodded that this was acceptable – just – and I paid and carried the drinks back to our table.

Lee reappeared and sat down. It hadn't really occurred to me that he would do a runner, though he easily could have as there was an exit from the staircase direct on to Cambridge Circus.

'Cheers,' sniffed Lee, downing the orange juice in one go.

I knew that licensees were told to watch out for strange behaviour from people returning from the toilets, in an effort to spot and stop drug taking. They were also trained to notice tell-tale signs such as the rapid consumption of soft drinks with large amounts of Vitamin C in them. I reckoned we were on borrowed time in this pub.

'So what do you know about Tigger, Lee? It's OK, you can tell me.'

'I'm not going to the funeral, you know. I don't do funerals.'

He picked a spent match out of the ashtray and began to snap it into small pieces.

'Nobody's going to make you do anything you don't want to,' I tried, in my second-best bedside manner. 'I just need to know what Tigger told you.'

'About what?' He was genuinely perplexed.

'I was hoping you'd tell me. Did he ever mention a guy called Bassotti?'

'I don't think so.'

'Hubbard?'

'I can't remember.'

'Did he ever talk about money? Did he ever give you any?'

'Tigger never had trouble getting money. Said he had lots of old friends who were always willing to lend a hand. He told me not to worry about where it came from. Told me not to worry at all. He said he'd take care of me.'

This was more painful than I had thought it would be.

'Did he mention money, bank accounts, a stash of cash somewhere? Where did he keep all his stuff?'

'What stuff?'

'His clothes, his CDs, his Filofax, I don't fucking know. His stuff, for Christ's sake.'

I thought he was going to cry again.

'He didn't have "stuff". He never had anything he wasn't able to carry around with him.'

'Look, Lee, I didn't mean to get ratty. Are you saying that Tigger never had a base camp anywhere? Come on, think. He must have had a stash of some sort.'

'Not that I know, honest.'

I felt near to tears myself by now.

'Listen, when Tigger and I worked together, he used to get his cut – his wages – and post them somewhere, every night.

Where would he be sending them, Lee? There must be an address . . . ?'

He thought about it hard, he really did. I could see the strain on his face.

'No, straight up, there was nowhere, nothing. He never said. He didn't even have a change of clothes. He just wore stuff then dumped it. If he liked things, he'd give them to people, like he gave me these trainers.'

We both looked down at Lee's feet.

'He gave you those?'

I had a mental flashback to Tigger, feet up on the dash of Bassotti's van then taking off one of his hi-tops and producing my wages from it like a rabbit from a hat.

'Yes,' said Lee. 'Told me to take special care of them as he might want them back. Of course, he never came back . . .'

'Get 'em off.'

'What?'

'Take 'em off, I want to have a look at them.'

He looked at me as if I had flipped then thought: Why not? It probably wasn't the weirdest offer he'd had that day.

He leant back in his chair and put both feet up on the table and began pulling at the long white laces.

That was when we got thrown out of the pub.

15

It was a key. Smaller than a house door key but bigger than, say, a briefcase lock or padlock key. And it had been hidden in the heel of Lee's right trainer quite simply by making a cut in the rubber where the heel sloped into the rest of the sole and sliding the key in. The pressure of the wearer's foot squeezed the rubber together to hide it and keep it in place, almost like the self-sealing tyres the Americans developed in Viet Nam.

But a key to what? And where? Lee didn't know and didn't really care much either. He was still trying to work out how I'd done the conjuring trick of finding the key. Neither did it strike him as odd to be standing on one foot leaning against the pedestrian railings in Cambridge Circus, handing over fifty per cent of his footwear to a virtual stranger while the rush hour crowd ebbed and flowed round him and the ticket touts began to pick their pitches for the evening performance of *Les Misérables*.

I handed Lee his hi-top and asked him one last question.

'Are you still using that tent in Lincoln's Inn for a berth?'

'Yeah,' he said, but shy all of a sudden. 'Unless, you know, something else comes up.'

'You could have chosen your words more carefully, but I know what you mean. What happens to the tent during the day?'

'One of the regulars looks after it for me. I do him . . . favours.' He looked at me, hurt. 'It'd get nicked otherwise.'

'You're right, it would. Did Tigger buy it for you?'

He nodded.

'I thought so. Did he pay cash?'

'Did, as a matter of fact. He was rolling in it a coupla weeks before . . . he . . . before . . .'

'Did he leave you any dosh?'

Lee smiled for the first time that afternoon; maybe that week.

'What, trust me with cash? He may have been a flake, but he wasn't fucking stupid.'

'Is a tenner any good to you?'

'Was Jesus a Jew?'

'Yes,' I said deadpan and waited as if for him to continue. I've found it the best way to deal with a smart-mouth.

'Er . . . I'm sorry. Yes, I could really use a tenner. Anything.'

I gave him a note and said: 'I'll be seeing you.' He bent down to fasten the laces on his trainer.

I headed back to where I'd left Armstrong on Denmark Street but cut across Charing Cross Road opposite the arcade where I'd found him. There was a bookshop with large, open, plate glass windows and I took up position there, pretending to browse through a biography of the twenty-seventh best-Prime-Minister-we-never-had-this-century.

Within a minute I spotted Lee turning into the arcade, waving the ten-pound note above his head.

I was glad I hadn't bothered to tell him to spend it wisely.

Rewind. Forward. Pause. Slow motion.

Something had bugged me from the start and that was Tigger's habit of posting his wages every night. I had no idea of the address and had never had a chance to catch him writing it as he always carried a pre-written, stamped envelope. But if that was how he made his deposits, there was something nagging me about how he made withdrawals. The connection, again, was Lee.

I replayed the scene in my mind when Tigger called me out from the dispatch company in order to pick up Lee. He had waved a wodge of twenty-pound notes at me and had said something to the effect that he'd got them from the 24-hour cash dispenser at the nearby bank on Seymour Street.

They are actually called ATMs – automated teller machines – but most people call them holes-in-the-wall or 'spits', because they spit money at you. Sometimes they don't, they just gobble up your card and leave you fuming and beating your head against the surrounding concrete. Ever wondered why they're always set in concrete? There had been a rash of spectacular thefts the year before where whole machines had been ripped out of the wall by mechanical diggers or small mobile cranes, usually early on a Friday night in the winter, when it was dark and the machine had been filled with cash for the weekend. And everyone knew the story – or saloon bar legend – of the gang who built a fake machine and waited for customers to stick their card in and enter their personal identification number, before swallowing the lot and nipping round the corner to the real ATM to make a rather large withdrawal.

Whatever their weaknesses, the one thing they don't do is spit out used and crumpled notes, because that would gum up the mechanism. And that's what Tigger had had that morning. There was also another reason I knew Tigger had been lying and that was the fact that the nearest bank only had ATMs inside, to take the pressure off the human tellers during peak periods. At the time I picked up Tigger, the bank's doors were still shut, so there was no way he could have used the machine there.

Of course he could have drawn the money out of a machine the day before, but everything about Tigger had suggested that he did not carry cash around if he could help it. So where had he got a fairly thick pile of notes at that time of the morning?

I reasoned that it had to be nearby and that necessitated a scouting patrol on foot.

I made it to Seymour Place just after six and parked up Armstrong in one of the mews off George Street. That meant I was halfway between Gloucester Place and the Edgware Road, with Marble Arch forming the tip of an upside-down triangle. I told myself I would start in that area and then work outwards. The one thing I couldn't tell myself was what the hell I was looking for.

I began by heading towards the Edgware Road and quartering back on myself through the area known as Little Beirut because of the density of Lebanese restaurants per square yard.

Nothing jumped out and bit me as a likely Tigger bolt hole or safe house, though I got some funny looks from a passing traffic warden, who caught me examining the drain covers of a Catholic church.

I hit the lucky button over towards Gloucester Place, in a side street behind the Churchill Hotel. The street had a pub and an Indian restaurant and a florist and an estate agent's and what we are now taught to call a 'convenience store' but at one time would have been described as the 'village shop' or the 'OAH' (Open All Hours).

This one was no different to a thousand other corner newsagents except that it had, instead of a shop window, a rank of mailboxes above which was a sign saying 'For Hire'.

I wandered over casually and began to read the 'Conditions of Hire' card which had been sellotaped to the front of box 1. The rates were reasonable. You paid a signing-on fee and then quarterly rental and for that you had confidentiality and 24-hour access to your personal mailbox, by use of your exclusive key (deposit: twenty-five pounds). Mail was addressed to the shop and sorted by name or box number into the boxes. You collected whenever you felt like it.

There were sixteen boxes in rows of four. While I was reading the instructions pinned to the first, I fumbled Tigger's key out of my pocket and, keeping my arm near my side, tried it in box 14, the second box in the bottom row. The lock wouldn't turn, but there was no doubt it was the right sort of key. I now had fifteen boxes to try but there was no way I was going to do that in broad daylight with the shop still open.

Which gave me an idea. I went inside and picked an *Evening Standard* off the counter, offering a pound coin to the dark-skinned lady behind the cash register.

'I've been looking at your rental boxes,' I charmed her. 'Got any spare ones, or are they all taken?'

'You have to fill in form,' she said, rooting around among

the circulars and bits of paper stuffed down the side of the till. 'And you have to pay deposit for key and a fee and the first rent in advance. But I haven't got any forms. Come back tomorrow.'

'Sure, but can you tell me if you've got one that's free?'

She scowled at this, but that was the trouble with customers – they kept wanting things.

She bent down behind the counter and came up holding a small, black tin cashbox. She opened it and removed a bunch of papers, most of which looked like unpaid telephone bills, and then came up with three keys, all identical to Tigger's, except these had numbered discs attached to the hole in the base of the key by safety pins.

'We got three to rent, looks like,' she said helpfully.

I leaned over and nodded in agreement, getting a good look at the numbers in the process.

'Well, one will do. Thanks. I'll pop back tomorrow. What time are you open?'

'We open seven to seven every day,' she said, taking away the need for my next question.

I smiled at her and left with my newspaper. It was only out on the street that I thought she might have been trying to get rid of me because I had been smiling my bruised and broken-cheeked leer. It obviously didn't work with some women.

I strode across the road without looking back at the shop, and into the Indian restaurant opposite. I ordered a King-fisher beer, a mild prawn curry, cottage cheese cooked in tomato sauce and rice instead of nan bread, because I reckoned that was as much as my teeth could handle.

As I was the first customer of the evening, I had no trouble getting a table near the window so I could watch the shop. Just before seven, the dark-skinned lady (Cypriot? Lebanese?) turned the lights off, locked up and left. On her way out she posted something through the slots in two of the mailboxes, numbers 4 and 7. I doubted if anyone was writing to Tigger here, so unless it was a reminder that his rent was overdue or similar, I thought it safe to assume that those two boxes were someone else's.

On the inside cover of a book of matches advertising the restaurant I drew four horizontal lines and three vertical ones to give me a grid for sixteen numbers. I wrote in numbers 4 and 7, then added 14, which I'd tried with Tigger's key. Then I put in the numbers of the three keys the shop lady had said were still free: 2, 8 and 9. That left me ten boxes to choose from. Ten-to-one were not the best odds I could wish for, but as I ate and drank another Kingfisher, two no-doubt scrupulously honest citizens going about their lawful business came along and improved the odds. One was a man in a sharp suit who left his Porsche parked half on the kerb as he opened box number 16. The mail almost fell out on to his brogues, there was so much in it. I put money on him running a reclaim scam. (You mailshot people saying that, for instance, five hundred pounds' worth of camera has been left at, say, Chicago O'Hare airport with their name on it and if *they* send fifteen pounds now to cover postage . . . well, you can guess the rest.) The other was a small Chinese girl who opened box number 11. I saw her shoulders sag and almost heard her sigh as she gazed into the empty box.

That brought the odds down to eight-to-one. Still not good, if anyone was looking and in view of the fact that there was a police station around the corner. Still, it had to be tried.

I paid the bill on a credit card in the name F. MacLean-Angel, which put me under 'M' in the computer instead of 'A'. Apart from that, it was a genuine card and the only one I had not up to my credit limit. It wasn't that the meal had been so good that I didn't mind paying for it, it was that I didn't want to give the restaurant any reason to remember me.

I said a cheery good-night to my waiter and as a party of four entered, I left and headed straight across the road. I had the key in my hand and in rapid succession, tried it in boxes 5 and 6.

No go. I risked one more, number 3, and again it refused to turn. At that point, a gang of young men fell noisily out of the nearby pub. I wasn't prepared to risk it, so I turned on my heel and set off back towards Armstrong.

It was now five-to-one and I felt confident that I could do

the lot under cover of Armstrong. I cut through the side streets and drew up outside the shop, mounting the pavement. Armstrong now effectively shielded me from passers-by, though I wondered why I was worried. I could probably have unscrewed the entire lot and taken them away in a truck without anyone noticing.

I left box number 1 as a last resort, as numbers 10, 12, 13 and 15 were lower down and out of sight behind Armstrong's gently idling engine. Ten and twelve were bad calls. Number 13 came up trumps.

Unlucky for some thirteen. It just had to be.

There were about a dozen envelopes in the box along with some sort of plastic sheets rolled up and secured with an elastic band. I grabbed the lot, hugging everything to my chest, locked the box and piled back into Armstrong.

I drove around Portman Square and cut across into Manchester Square, parking on an empty meter. Only then did I start to sift through my booty.

All the envelopes except one contained money. All were addressed to 'A. A. Milne' care of box 13 at the accommodation address. Nice one, Tigger, taking your creator's name in vain.

Some of the envelopes had postmarks from a year before. Some of the more recent ones hadn't even been opened. They were addressed in a mixture of handwriting and typing and while most of the postmarks were London, there were two from Reading, one from Norwich and one from Canterbury. They all had sums of at least fifty pounds or a hundred pounds in used notes, mostly twenties, except the most recent of all which was a brown foolscap envelope bearing a commercial postmark rather than a stamp. That one had been slit open and positively bulged with twenty-pound notes; on a quick flick count, about two thousand pounds.

Two of the stamped, hand-written envelopes contained slips of paper as well as cash. On one, a pink piece of card the size of a visiting card, was scribbled: 'Call me. Please.' On the other, a sheet of cheap writing paper, was written: 'Tigger, this is the last. No more.' Neither was signed.

One envelope did not contain cash. That one held a building society passbook showing that C. R. O'Neil had an instant access account with a credit balance of £11,953. I had not only found Tigger's own personal hole-in-the-wall machine, but his life savings as well. And there were no prizes for guessing how he had come by these voluntary donations.

Except the latest and biggest. I peered at the franking machine stamp. Somebody had been careless, sending blackmail money through the office post. Although maybe they had been pretty sure they could recover it. Somebody at H.B. Builders, that is.

I dug into my wallet and found the slip of headed notepaper which Bert Bassotti had given me bearing the company's phone number. I hadn't looked at it closely enough before now, but under the bit which said 'Registered House Builder' came, in very small print, the names of the directors: U. Bassotti, E. Bassotti, L. Hubbard.

The 'H.B.' stood for Hubbard and Bassotti, partners in more than just the building game. What was it I'd heard down in Nether World? 'Mr Hubbard said no marks, Sammy' — something like that. I hadn't met Mr Hubbard and it seemed sensible to keep things that way.

But partners in what? Illegal fly-tipping was, well, illegal, but hardly a reason to cough up two grand in blackmail. Or reason enough to kill somebody.

There was one package I still had not opened, the roll of plastic material rather like the tape the police stretch across the road when there's been an accident. Except this wasn't a roll, it was a bundle of adhesive notices about the same size and shape as a car bumper sticker. They had all been used, the backing sheets ripped off them, and several were stuck together with what remained of the adhesive.

They all said the same thing: HAZCHEM — BIOLOGICAL WASTE — AUTHORIZED DISPOSAL ONLY.

Suddenly I didn't want to touch the money any more.

Fenella was waiting in ambush on the stairs outside her flat when I got back to Stuart Street.

'Angel, I just had to tell you,' she whispered, having put a finger to her lips to tell me to be quiet. 'Mr Goodson thinks

I should put in for my driving test. What have you got inside your jacket?'

'Oh, nothing, just some papers. Did he say when?'

'Well, he thinks there's quite a waiting list and it might be a year or more before I get a test.'

'That's nice.'

'But he thinks I should go to a driving school and get professional lessons.'

'Good idea.' Mr Goodson was not as daft as I'd thought.

'But if I do that it will mean staying here and not moving to the country. I don't know how to break it to Lisabeth.'

I eased my way around her and continued up the stairs.

'Where is she, anyway? I haven't seen her for days.'

'Her circadian rhythms are out of step,' she hissed.

'Her what?'

'Circadian body rhythms. You know, your biological clock which has twenty-five hours in the day. Well she's got this notion that her clock is slow and she's having to put in twenty-six hours a day, so she needs her sleep.'

'I won't argue,' I said quietly, 'not while oxygen is still precious.'

'I think she'd miss the city, anyway,' Fenella said, more or less to herself. 'She's really a town mouse at heart.'

'It's the rats you have to worry about,' I said, but I don't think she heard.

Inside my flat, I locked the door behind me and went into the bedroom. Leaning over the bed, I unzipped my leather jacket and all of Tigger's envelopes fell out on to the duvet.

I sorted most of the money and the building society passbook to one side and loaded five twenty-pound notes into my wallet as I fetched my special edition of Hugh Brogan's *History of the United States* from the bookshelf.

As part repayment of a debt some years ago, an acquaintance known as Lenny the Lathe had converted the book into a metal, fireproof, miniature safe, complete with combination lock. I referred to it occasionally as my War Chest but times had been so thin of late I was just glad there wasn't a war on.

I crammed the money and passbook in and spun the small

wheel to lock the combination. The envelopes I tore into shreds and scattered them in Springsteen's litter tray along with a fresh sprinkling of non-mineral, biodegradable, pine-scented, recycled, absorbent wood chips. He rarely used the tray, but let's face it, who would go rooting around in there for evidence?

I stripped off most of my clothes and put on the black T-shirt I had worn down in Nether World and which Fenella had washed for me, along with some black brushed cotton trousers and dark blue, canvas deck shoes. So it wasn't an ensemble to be seen in; but that was the point.

The T-shirt reminded me of Nether World and the fact that I had left my torch down there somewhere, so I decided to borrow one from Doogie upstairs.

He answered the door himself but behind him I could see Miranda sitting cross-legged on the floor packing things into a cardboard box.

'Hullo, Angel. What's up? Going burgling?'

'Can't fool you, Doogie, but I thought I'd knock and see if you had anything worth nicking first. No, look, I've got to do some running repairs on Armstrong and I'm buggered if I can find a torch. Would you have the loan of one?'

He gave me his tough-guy look, which for him comes naturally.

'As long as I get it back this time.'

'What have I borrowed that you never got back?' I asked, hurt.

'Two corkscrews, a wine cooler and three-quarters of a bottle of malt whisky.'

'That was a party.' I was indignant. 'Parties don't count.'

'Hah!' He stalked off into his kitchen.

Miranda smiled up at me.

'You were right, Angel,' she said softly.

I don't know which surprised me more, her smiling or me being accused of being right.

'About what?'

'About our move to Scotland. Doogie has his heart set on it, but I wouldn't be happy playing the wee lassie tending the hearth.'

I suddenly realized she was unpacking, not packing.

'So I'm not going with him.'

'How's he taking it? And you didn't say I had anything to do with this, did you?'

'He's reconsidering,' she said primly. 'Which means he'll stay with me. We'd both miss London if the truth were told. We'd miss the excitement, the big city life.'

'Yeah, it's just a barrel of fun isn't it?'

Doogie reappeared with a black plastic torch.

'Just twist the head to turn it on,' he said. 'I've counted the batteries.'

'Don't panic, you'll get it back in the morning.'

He produced something from behind his back.

'And you might as well borrow this.'

It was a black woollen bobble hat and he pulled it over my hair until it covered my ears.

'There,' he said. 'Now you look the part.'

16

Rewind. Pause. Fast forward.

I almost had it all now. Things I should have noticed at the time but failed to. Or maybe I did but just blotted them out. Like the fact that every time Tigger and I picked up a van on Bassotti's instructions, it would be parked within half a mile of a hospital.

On the way over to Globe Town I stopped at a 7–11 convenience store and bought a pair of extra-strength washing-up gloves.

You can never be too careful.

Someone had repaired the broken gate at Hubbard's Yard and they had thoughtfully added a new padlock and hasp. So that ruled out the front door.

I drove slowly along the perimeter fence and chose my spot, then I ditched Armstrong around a corner out of sight. I carried only Doogie's torch and Armstrong's keys with me, leaving anything which could identify me locked in the glove compartment. I zippered Armstrong's keys into the inside pocket of my jacket and pulled on the rubber kitchen gloves, pulling a pair of black leather gloves on top.

The double glove felt cumbersome but I tested my grip on the large-mesh wire fence and found I could hold well enough. At my chosen spot, I reached up and grabbed the wire, hauling myself up and digging the toes of my canvas shoes in to get purchase. The fence wasn't that high, perhaps ten feet, but it had a single strand of barbed wire running along the top. I negotiated that but for a second lay along the top of the wire, swaying wildly.

The reason I had picked this spot, though, was because on

the other side of the fence was the nearest pile of junked cars. There were three on top of each other and I had only to reach out a hand to grab the door handle of a gutted, partially crushed Ford pick-up to pull myself over and into the back of the truck. From there I could look down on to the empty street and the rest of the yard, stretching beyond the avenues of wrecked vehicles and into the darkness where the canal must be.

The large brick shed was still padlocked and on its corners the two fake video cameras − at least according to Tigger − flashed their little red lights to the night sky just to show their batteries were working. I knew enough to keep near the line of wrecked cars to avoid the movement-sensitive lights, and anyway, that was where I was hoping to find whatever it was I was looking for.

The last time Tigger and I had been here he had dumped six bags of something from the van. But unlike the first trip, he had not gone as far as the canal and I had distinctly heard him crashing around among the wrecked cars. He had not had a torch, so whatever he had stashed would be in one of the first rank of wrecks, which in some cases were stacked five high and seven or eight deep.

I lowered myself over the side of the pick-up and dropped gingerly to the ground. Taking Doogie's torch from inside my jacket, I tried the beam on an experimental basis. It was like a searchlight and a dead giveaway to any curious passers-by.

I congratulated myself on thinking ahead and took a roll of black insulating tape from my pocket, ripping off four pieces to reduce the face area of the torch to a one-inch square. That gave me a powerful pencil beam which was far more controllable and less noticeable from outside the yard.

From where I guessed I had parked the van that time with Tigger, I walked about thirty yards until I was opposite the far end of the brick building. That, I estimated, was the earliest point Tigger would have dumped anything.

The nearest pile of wrecks contained a Ford Thames van, a Triumph Toledo squashed to a thickness of no more than a foot, the rear end of a Vauxhall of some sort and a chassis and frame of what might once have been a Fiat. I flicked the torch beam up and down the pile and decided there was no way anything other than a single cigarette paper could be inserted into such a twisted mass of metal.

The second row looked more promising, with a pair of Renault saloons sandwiched between an old London Electricity Board van and a crushed Skoda. The Renaults both pointed the same way and their bodies seemed more or less intact, although all the wheels were missing, as probably the engines were too.

I stood on the remains of the Skoda and shone the torch in the back window of the lower Renault. There was nothing in there, not even seats, and neither of the doors on my side would open.

I reached up to the Renault above and tried the back door handle more in hope than expectation. I was surprised when it opened and horrified when something black and bulky fell towards me at head height.

It was one of Tigger's black plastic sacks. I knew it had to be but it still scared the hell out of me. I suppose it was because I was powerless to stop it falling on me, with one hand on the car door handle and the other holding the torch.

I tried to ward it off and discovered it was not as heavy as it looked. But by that time I had missed my footing on the Skoda and was falling backwards conscious only of a frantic need to protect the right side of my face from further damage. I didn't have far to fall but I managed to do it as awkwardly as possible, the back of my head taking the brunt of the impact as I bounced off one of the neighbouring wrecks. My foot caught on a jagged spear of metal and I felt my sock rip and a searing pain and after that it just seemed easier to flop down on my backside.

The black plastic dustbin bag was at my feet and I stared at it as I shook my head gently and rubbed my bleeding right ankle.

I shone Doogie's torch at it but it didn't move. I shone the torch up towards the Renault where the back door was still open. Through it I could see several other black sacks.

The one at my feet had a heavy-duty wire twist clip around

its neck. I wondered if the others did. I wondered how much longer I could put off opening one of the damn things.

I got to my knees and holding the torch in my left hand, I began to untwist the wire clip around the sack which had fallen on me. Half a dozen turns and it fell away and the sack opened to reveal another black sack with a wire clip inside.

I tore into that one and pulled it off, ripping the bag in the process. There was enough light without the torch to see that the sack contained hundreds of used hypodermic syringes.

I never knew before then just how fast I could travel backwards whilst still on my knees.

There were hundreds of them; thousands altogether. And — oh, God — there were used swabs and bits of cotton wool with blood spots . . . Just some harmless, non-toxic industrial waste, eh? Next time, let's be really socially responsible and dump the stuff on a playground or maybe in a school yard.

And Tigger, of all people, must have known. And not only known, but was prepared to make capital out of it by blackmail either of Bassotti or Hubbard or, knowing Tigger, probably both. Bassotti had cracked when it got nasty. Hubbard just got nasty.

Hence the HAZCHEM adhesive signs in Tigger's dead letter box. Bassotti and Hubbard — or why not Hubbard/Bassotti as in H.B. Builders? — must have got themselves some sort of licensed franchise to collect the bio-waste from various hospitals on a promise to incinerate it. But incinerators cost money; fly-tipping is cheaper.

The vans would have done the hospital runs and then they were parked up and the official signs peeled off — they were easy enough to get printed up on crack-back plastic — awaiting some likely mug like me to come and do the driving. Goodness knows how many trips they'd done before I joined the outfit, or how long Tigger had been screwing them for extra cash. I could only hazard a guess that the racket was sufficiently large scale to warrant killing Tigger. Or maybe it was small scale and they were just bastards.

I still didn't want to touch the open sack and I had no

specific ideas what to do next, when my mind was made up for me.

I heard the engine but didn't really register it until it stopped and idled and I realized it was outside the yard gate. I poked my head around one of the wrecks and could see fingers of light from its headlights stabbing through the holes and cracks and around the hinges in the gates.

Shit!

I grabbed the sack by the neck and dragged it around the back of the first row of wrecks. The gates were opening now, I could hear them creaking, and headlight beams were illuminating the yard.

As the lights got nearer, I remembered to go back and close the door of the Renault, forcing the bags in there back inside. And it was then I realized what Tigger had been up to on that last run. He had planted these six bags in Hubbard's own yard and as they were still there, he hadn't told anyone about them. So he was planning to blow the whistle on the racket, though not before he had increased the size of his nest egg.

I risked another look. It was a white Transit van and it had parked outside the padlocked brick building. A dark-coloured Jaguar had followed it.

Sure enough, the van had a sign on its side: HAZCHEM – BIOLOGICAL WASTE – AUTHORIZED DISPOSAL ONLY.

The driver let his engine idle again and opened his door. I saw his shadow in the headlights as he walked across the beams and as he approached the brick building, the sensor lights on the walls came on.

I could see him from behind, a short guy, walking into the light as if from a scene in a Seventies sci-fi movie.

From behind him I heard an electric car window go down and then a voice: 'Have you got the keys, Sammy?'

The short guy raised an arm and yelled, without looking round: 'Sure thing, Mister Aitch.'

Sammy opened the doors of the brick building, returned to the van and drove it inside. He didn't bother turning on any lights inside, he just switched off the engine, locked up and came out and began closing the doors.

The driver of the Jag, Mr H., had switched off too and I

could hear Sammy grunt pushing the doors. Sammy would lock them, get in the Jag and drive away. That's what I reckoned would happen. Why else would anyone want to spend good drinking time or quality TV time hanging around a scrap yard in east London?

'Don't rush, Sammy,' came the voice from the Jaguar. 'I'll give the dogs a bit of a run.'

Oh fuck.

I moved as quickly as I could into the maze of wrecks, conscious of the need to be quiet now there were no engines running and not even a passing train to mask the noise of my stumblings.

I used the torch because I was frightened of impaling myself on a sharpened Lada axle or similar, the car's last act of revenge for being crushed or scrapped. So I kept the beam pointed down and close to my body, allowing only a small pool of light for my feet to follow.

When I was three rows of wrecks into the forest of metal I tried to pick a route left. It was easy enough to keep my bearings, just head away from the light. Eventually I must come to either the scrubland and the canal or the railway line. The trouble was that even at this depth in – only three car lengths – the wrecks had tipped and tilted or been shoved closer together so that in some cases it was impossible to squeeze between the piles.

I heard a deep bark and it seemed far too close for comfort. Then the voice from the Jaguar saying: 'What's up, Simba? Spotted a rat have we?'

Why did he have to give the stupid animal ideas?

There was only one thing for it, I had to go up and over and just hope that I had enough wrecks between me and Sammy and Co. to keep me hidden.

Thankful for the gloves, I pulled myself up on to the roof of a Volvo which had seen happier days. From there I jumped on to the bonnet of half an Alfa Romeo and from there, up slightly on to the roof of what appeared to have been an ice-cream van at some time.

From behind, and lower, came another bark, then a

second, from over to my left. Of course, the sod had said dogs – plural.

'What is it, Simba? Go on, boy, seek!' came the voice. I was beginning to take against him.

But the sound which frightened me most was the scrabble of doggy claws on metal. One of the beasts had worked out that the quickest way through a junkyard was up and was trying to get purchase.

I risked the torch out in front of me. Three more rows of cars and then darkness. A Ford, something so beaten I couldn't recognize it and then a Fiat. A mere hop, skip and a jump.

From close, too close, behind me came a deep 'Woof!' but I didn't look back. I jumped and jumped again, knowing that if I slipped, Simba's sister or brother or live-in doggy lover would be waiting to pick up the pieces.

There wasn't time to use the torch when I hit the roof of the Fiat; I just leapt on into space, landing hard but not falling, still moving. I hadn't time to worry about being out of breath or unfit. No time to regret that last cigarette. I had twin Dobermans on my tail, or maybe pit bulls or Irish wolfhounds. And I was running out of space.

I saw light reflecting on the water of the canal, but whether it was moonlight or reflections from the nearby block of flats, I didn't know and couldn't care.

At the edge, I turned around for the first time. Simba, if that was he, was on top of one of the wreck piles, silhouetted like he was auditioning for the *Hound of the Baskervilles*. He wasn't a Doberman, so that was OK. He was a German Shepherd and his sister, or whoever, had come around the piles of scrap and was heading for me like a bullet. Clever doggy.

I didn't think about it, I just lowered myself over the bank and dropped down into the dank waters. I was scared but not stupid enough to jump into water you can't see through. (Rule of Life No. 124, and that includes jacuzzis.)

Doogie's torch went to the bottom straightaway, but I had other things to worry about. Such as keeping my head out of the water, which was not only cold but almost certainly riddled with typhus. Such as laying odds on whether the dogs fancied a moonlight swim. Such as wondering where the hell the Grand Union Canal came out anyway. In a sewage works or off the coast of France?

I sculled backwards, keeping to the scrap-yard side and I had made about ten feet before the first dog appeared, leaning over but not wanting to come in and contenting itself with a volley of barking.

From beyond I could hear: 'Simba, come here you thick bugger! It's only a rat. Leave it now. Heel!'

Go on, Simba, I willed, looking him in his gleaming dead eyes. You heard your master. Piss off and leave us rats in peace.

Then dog number two appeared as well and the volume of barking went up by sixty watts per channel.

I sculled some more, trying to raise as little wake in the water as possible. The dogs didn't seem to want to follow me along the bank. They stayed at the spot where I had slid in. Maybe they just didn't want to get wet. Maybe they were amateurs at this game and really just chasing me for a bit of exercise. They had barked, of course, and no decent attack dog ever lets you know it's coming. They were just puppies. The hell with that. They were the ones with full sets of teeth.

'Simba, Darlene, will you get the fuck back here?'

Yeah, go on, do it, you animals. Darlene? Christ, no wonder the bitch had an attitude.

'Start the car, Sammy, that usually brings them.'

Do it, Sammy, don't dawdle. Turn the key and fire up the Jag, I'm getting cramp here.

I was twenty feet away and treading water carefully when I heard the voice very close.

'Come on, you two, you've had your run.'

I heard a clicking sound, like a lead being clipped on to a collar.

'Let's get you home to Mummy.'

Yeah, go on, Fang, go home. Mummy will have your pound of red meat waiting for you.

'Darlene, come here, will you? Bad girl, heel!'

Darlene wasn't the giving-up type. She couldn't resist one

last look over the edge of the canal and she came so close that I could smell her doggy breath. I hugged the bank, which had been lined with wooden posts to prevent erosion, though most of the wood was now well rotted and eroding itself.

'Darlene! Heel!'

Darlene and I were staring each other out, me scarcely daring to breathe. She curled a soft black lip over her side teeth and growled quietly at me. I did the same to her without the growl and she looked at me curiously, head on one side.

Behind me somewhere there was a plopping sound in the water.

'There, I told you it was rats,' said the voice. 'Now sit!'

There was a click as a lead snapped on.

'Now, let's go, you daft animal.'

But Darlene, typical woman, couldn't let it lie. She strained over the banking tugging the lead and whoever was holding it into view.

I thanked Doogie for lending me the black bobble cap, took a deep breath, closed my eyes, and went under.

Using touch only, and precious little of that through the two pairs of gloves, I tried to work my way along the bank by clawing at the wooden planking. I did this for about three hours and estimated that I'd moved nearly two feet. Actually, it was probably no more than thirty seconds, but I was right about the two feet.

The worst thing of all was coming up slowly and breaking the oily surface as quietly as possible. When I did open my eyes, there was no sign of the dog, but a pair of rats not much smaller were scampering along the edge of the banking, about six inches from my face.

The man with the dogs had been right, there was nobody down here but us rats.

I saw the headlights of the Jaguar swing through the night sky above me as it turned round. Then I listened until I was sure someone had closed the gates and the engine noise had disappeared into the distance.

I was hanging on to the banking now, too tired to tread water, and feeling for purchase so I could haul myself out.

My clothes weighed a ton and I had convinced myself that I had taken in canal water, typhus and bubonic plague bacilli in equal parts.

Right then I would have settled for a nice quiet life in front of the television. Go home, get dry, have a drink or three, forget all about Tigger and Bassotti and Hubbard and dogs and unthinkable piles of hospital waste carelessly scattered over who knew how much of the city.

What was it Doc had said? Life didn't suck, just the people in it. I wasn't sure she was right.

My right hand found something to hang on to, the edge of a plank at a part of the bank where three or four planks bulged out into the water. I put both hands on the top edge of a pair of planks and pulled myself up, scrabbling for a toehold as I went. I had my forearms over the edge when the planks started to crumble under my weight.

I reached out wildly and grabbed a gloveful of mud. I lunged again and this time came away with something altogether different.

As the banking planks gave way and I pitched back into the slimy water, I realized that what I had been trying to grip was a black plastic dustbin bag just like the ones in the wrecked car. I had found where Tigger had dumped the rest of the sacks. Not in the canal itself but, either by accident or design, down the side of the planking which shored up the bank.

The one I had a hold of came with me and ripped open as I fell backwards, pulling it over the rough wood. The bag burst and I hit the water in a shower of plastic hypodermics.

I remember thinking that screaming wasn't a good idea as it involved opening my mouth, but I have no recollection of swimming through that ghastly flotsam or of climbing out of the canal with a speed and strength born of desperation.

I stood on the bank dripping wet and cold and looking down on at least half a dozen more sacks uncovered behind the rotting planks.

Now I was really pissed off.

17

It could have been the sight of the syringes floating up to form a bizarre, bobbing scum on the surface of the canal which pushed me over the edge; seeing the red mist.

I pulled two of the bags out of the banking and tore the wire seals from them. One I carried, the other I dragged so that the contents spilled out in a trail behind me. When one sack was empty, I tipped up the second, leaving a trail from the canal to the middle of the scrap yard.

I slipped and scrambled over the wrecks to get at the bags I had found earlier. I ripped those open and scattered the contents in front of the building where Sammy had hidden the Transit. I think I might have been crying by the time I dragged the last bag, the one I'd hidden, out from under the wrecks and I used the contents of that one to lay a trail right up to the front gates.

The security lights in the yard were still on, probably working on a timer arrangement. As I climbed up the pile of wrecks nearest the fence, I looked back across the yard and saw the unholy twinkling of a thousand shiny needles and felt sure that Tigger would have approved.

I half fell over the fence and I heard something rip as I cleared the barbed wire, but I was past caring. I pulled off my right glove by holding it between my knees and then peeled off the rubber one underneath. I dug Armstrong's key out of my jacket and squelched into the seat, firing up the engine and cranking the heater up to maximum.

I didn't even glance at Hubbard's Yard as I drove by. Two streets later I found what I was looking for, a phone box.

I still had gloves on my left hand, which held the receiver, and I used the knuckle of my right index finger to press the nine button three times.

When they asked which emergency service I required, I said, 'Police,' and there was a pause while they put me through and made sure the tape-recorder was running.

They asked who I was and where I was phoning from. I said my name was Christopher Robin O'Neil and I was in a phone box near Hubbard's scrap yard off Roman Road in Globe Town.

'And what exactly is the problem, sir?'

'I want to report a serious health hazard.'

Three days later, after a dozen baths to take away the smell and taste of the canal, I found Lee early one morning down at Lincoln's Inn.

He was walking out of the Fields, his dome tent rolled up and slung over his shoulder. A supermarket carrier bag seemed to contain everything else he owned.

I slowed down and signalled him to get in the back of Armstrong. He stood bemused for a minute until he recognized me.

'I've got something for you,' I said as I pulled over to the kerb. 'Something I think Tigger would have wanted you to have.'

I held the building society passbook out to him through the cab's sliding glass partition. He had to let go of his tent and carrier bag to take it. He was beginning to trust me.

'What is it?' He opened it and saw the money I had placed inside.

'It's Tigger's building society book. If you look in the back there's a sample of his signature. Learn how to do it and you can get up to three hundred pounds in cash at one go. That's what I did. But don't use any of the branch offices in the West End. The odds are that he opened the account up west and they're not likely to forget him, are they?'

'You got this?' It was all too much for him. Literally, he thought. 'But I can't take it. It's too much.'

'There's over eleven grand in there, Lee. Take it out gently or get them to do you a big cheque and open your own bank

189

account. Just remember to sign things C. R. O'Neil and don't be greedy. It could keep you going for months, maybe years.'

'No, you don't get it.' He looked at me wide-eyed. 'It's too much at one go. I can't be trusted. I promised Doc . . .'

'What would you feel happier with?'

'Twenty, thirty.' Not enough for a big fix in other words.

'Then give it here.'

I took most of the notes out of the book, leaving him with four ten-pound notes.

'There's forty. Are you sure?'

'Yeah, that's better. That's manageable, man. No temptation.' He did genuinely seem happier. 'And anyway, you need something for your trouble, don't you?'

I looked up and down the street. 'I'm taken care of,' I said, thinking about the stash of cash back at Stuart Street. 'Keep the book.'

'What if they catch me forging Tigger's name?'

'Tell them he gave it to you and then disappeared, or just say you found it. What the hell *can* they do to you?'

He cheered up at that.

'Hey, you're right. I'm still a minor. Not legally responsible for my actions. Isn't that cool, or what?'

'Yeah, cool.'

It was another week before the story hit the newspapers, or, at least, the London ones.

Doc told me about it as we shared a cigarette while sprawled across the sofa bed in her flat. Smoking was the second politically incorrect thing we'd done that afternoon.

Police were holding two men, and looking for a third, in connection with illegal dumping of medical waste and pending possible corruption charges to do with contracts for refuse disposal from various local councils. The two men had not been named as yet but bail had been refused as there was reason to believe the men would abscond, just as Bassotti had.

Unusually, reporting restrictions were partly lifted in that the cops were anxious to locate the dumping grounds of the scam which, it was suggested, had been going on for over a year. Warnings were being broadcast and posters printed telling people to watch out for black plastic bags tied with wire seals, but not to touch them at any cost.

'No mention of any link with Tigger,' said Doc.

'Somebody may put two and two together eventually,' I said. 'Or maybe they already have but are just keeping it under wraps. If they find Bassotti, he'll talk. He's not the sort to go down quietly and I never really saw him as condoning the rough stuff. He was being used by Hubbard.'

'Like you were used?' she asked gently.

'Sure, like me. They used me to find Tigger. There, I've said it. Does it make me feel any better? No. Should I give back the thirty pieces of silver they offered? Would that help Tigger? I doubt it.'

'Don't get heavy, Angel, I was only trying to figure out why you did what you did.'

'Well figure away. Are you doing psychiatry on the side as well?'

'No, I'm not,' she snapped angrily, then thought about it. 'As well as what?'

'Never mind. Have you formed any conclusions then? About my behaviour, I mean?'

'Well, from what you've told me, there was an affinity with Tigger which you always denied.'

'That's bollocks. He might have thought that, but I never did.'

'Hmmm. Denied violently, it seems,' she murmured. 'So you didn't see Tigger as another side of your personality?'

'Where do you get this stuff? There's a couple of ladies I house share with would like the book when you've finished with it.'

'Classic macho rejection syndrome. Is this because Tigger was gay?'

'Oh, I see. If I don't accept that Tigger was the dark side of my personal force it's because I'm homophobic, is that it?'

She sat up, naked, and held a clenched fist in front of my face.

'Right then, let's stop playing Nice Doctor, Nasty Doctor.

Tell me what your motive was or the orthodontist will have twice as much rebuilding to do tomorrow.'

'That's it, fight dirty. You know I'm scared of dentists.'

I pushed her gently away and rolled over to stub out the cigarette in the coffee-jar lid she used as an ashtray.

'I didn't do it because of any weird personality bonding with Tigger. Don't fool yourself that Tigger felt anything for me or anybody else, except maybe Lee. And I didn't do it to avenge him either. He was involved in a dirty business, a very dirty business, and one where he of all people knew the nastiness in those bags. But he was also a blackmailer and he took on the big boys and he lost.

'And I didn't even do it particularly because I was conned into playing the Judas and leading them to him. He'd got himself into the shit without my help.'

Doc looked genuinely interested.

'So why? Why did you set them up and drop the dime on them, calling the cops? You didn't have to. Why?'

'Like you once said, Doc, somebody had to.'